The Stockton Saga 2

The Stockton Saga 2
Star of Justice

Steven Douglas Glover

iUniverse, Inc.
Bloomington

The Stockton Saga 2
Star of Justice

iUniverse books may be ordered through booksellers or by contacting:

iUniverse
1663 Liberty Drive
Bloomington, IN 47403
www.iuniverse.com
1-800-Authors (1-800-288-4677)

ISBN: 978-1-4620-5314-8 (sc)
ISBN: 978-1-4620-5315-5 (ebk)

Printed in the United States of America

iUniverse rev. date: 09/09/2011

CONTENTS

PREFACE

The Stockton Saga began as a short story for a friend. She liked the story so much that I decided to write another—a follow up to it, and that progressed into yet another. I seemed to have no end to stories about my main character, Cole Stockton. Reviews by a select group of readers asked for longer, more detailed stories and subsequently, they formed an entire series.

It was relayed to me that if you took all the Cole Stockton stories and put them together that they formed a novel. With that thought in mind, I decided to publish *The Stockton Saga: Dawn of the Gunfighter*, which tells of Cole's early life and the elements that formed his mystique.

This story, *The Stockton Saga 2: Star of Justice*, picks up where *Dawn of the Gunfighter* leaves off, and continues the story of Cole Stockton, gunfighter, and now Deputy U.S. Marshal within the Colorado Territory. This story also introduces the character of Laura Lynne Sumner, who will become memorable to all who read this series. I have been told that the combination of Cole and Laura is mesmerizing.

I try to portray the old west as it really was, lending authenticity to wherever possible. When I include historical characters, my physical descriptions are as researched. When I speak of a certain weapon, pistol or rifle, I've researched to the aspect that it was indeed available at that time.

In all cases, my stories are purely fictional. I build characters within the recesses of my mind—any similarity to an actual person is purely coincidental. My stories are written for enjoyment only and are not intended to be historically accurate by date, incident, or actual person.

Immeasurable appreciation goes to Monti Lynne Eastin for the psyche of the character Laura Sumner, as well as her invaluable reviews of my short stories. Monti also provided assistance with specific information about various types of horses. Her support in the writing of my stories and continuous prompting to publish them endears her as an all time *Best Friend*.

My immense gratitude goes to Gay Lynn Auld whose time and effort provided immeasurable assistance in reviewing and editing this manuscript. Her suggestions for expansion and rewrite proved invaluable to the production of this book.

A special thanks to Linda Glover, without whose review and moral support this book would not have been published.

Very special thanks to Verna Glover, Mary Hughes, Lois Weller, and Helen Werner—my dedicated fans who mentioned time and time again, that I should publish these stories.

Steven Douglas Glover
Round Rock, Texas
August 27, 2011

"The Stockton Saga 2; Star Of Justice"

Dedicated To The Memory Of My Good Friend; An Avid Fan
Of My Western Stories.

Dode Offord
Dec 2, 1921-Jan 5, 2011

And To The Memory Of

Louis L'amour
1908-1988

CHAPTER ONE

The Star Of Justice

I had just spent several months tracking down Charlie Sturgis, a vicious killer who attempted to ambush me in the New Mexico Territory. Crisscrossing the southwest as I followed his path of death and destruction, I finally caught up with him at a saloon in Las Cruces, New Mexico Territory. The gunfight that followed put an end to Charlie's reign of terror. It was then that Deputy United States Marshal George Jamison insisted that I accompany him to meet a judge in the Colorado Territory. I had no further immediate business to attend to, and was curious to learn what a federal judge would want of me. I traveled with him to the wilds of Colorado.

Leaving our horses at the hitching rack in front of the two-story Denver courthouse, Jamison led me to the second floor. Entering a door with *Territorial District Court* etched on the glass, Jamison informed the somber fellow behind the desk that we were there to see the judge. "Henry," he added, "we don't want to keep the judge waiting." Henry nodded his understanding and stuck his head into the judge's office, announcing our arrival. We were ushered in forthwith.

Judge Joshua Bernard Wilkerson rose from behind his large oak desk as we entered the room, then lumbered around to the front of it. He took my hand with a firm grip and exuberantly pumped it up and down while surveying my lanky six-foot frame and blue-green eyes. The judge himself stood about six foot two with steel-gray eyes and a preacher-like smile. I rather liked him from the start.

"Cole Stockton!" he exclaimed. "Welcome to Denver. I am glad to finally make your acquaintance. Come. Sit down and we'll talk a bit."

He motioned me to one of the comfortable chairs in front of his desk while Marshal Jamison took the other. Judge Wilkerson sat back on the edge of his desk and placed his arms across his chest. He thoughtfully held my gaze as he pondered his next statement, "Mr. Stockton, I suppose that you would like to know why I brought you here." I nodded my acknowledgement to that fact.

Judge Wilkerson's eyes turned serious and he pursed his lips somewhat before continuing. "Mr. Stockton, I have followed your doings and derring-do for quite some time now and I have to tell you that I cannot allow a man of your obvious knowledge and skill to continue gallivanting all over the countryside and shooting people."

He paused while he stretched backward across his desk to draw open the center drawer. After rummaging around for a moment or so, he pulled his hand out. A moment later, he placed a silver Deputy U.S. Marshal star on the desk in front of me, and continued with, "That is, unless you wear this."

My eyes riveted on the star for an instant as a strange feeling surged through my being.

Wilkerson continued to talk, "Cole, the Colorado Territory is plagued with all sorts of rascals, murderers, thieves, and others of dubious repute. There has been talk of statehood and many want to see it. There are others, however, that do not. If the lawlessness is not curtailed, we will never become a state of the Union. I have been empowered to form a group of dedicated law officers to clean up this territory. I want you as one of my marshals. Will you accept the job? You will answer only to this court. The pay is fifty dollars a month, plus rewards, writ serving fees, and all the bullets you need."

Having said his piece, Judge Wilkerson studied me as I pondered a decision. My mind surged through the portals of my life as I thought of those whom I had dispatched with swift and deadly action. I thought of my personal creed—to use my gun only in self-defense and for those who needed justice. Wearing *The Star* meant not having to sell my gun to outfits anymore. It meant a real job. I saw the means to do good for people and I surely wanted that. Slowly, I rose from the chair, reached down, and pinned the star on my shirt.

Marshal Jamison stood witness as the judge held a Bible out to me. I placed my left hand on it while raising my right to repeat the statement that bound my word and soul to the law. "I, Cole

Stockton, do hereby swear to uphold the laws of *The Constitution*, and to protect—so help me God."

The judge grinned widely as he shook my hand once more proclaiming, "Welcome to our side, Marshal Stockton." Jamison also shook my hand as he nodded approvingly.

"Marshal Jamison, take our newest Marshal over to Ma Sterling's boarding house and get him situated with a place to stay. Tomorrow, I would like for the two of you to meet with me at eight in the morning. I received word this very day that the outlaw leader Frank Murphy was captured. He is being held in the Fort Collins County Jail. Sheriff Latimer is worried that his gang may try to spring him from the jaws of justice and has requested a U.S. Marshal to bring him here for safekeeping. The man will ultimately be tried in my court. The earlier we get him in our clutches the better it will be."

Jamison and I bid the Judge good day, then stepped out to the street. Mounting our horses, I posed the question. "Who is Frank Murphy? I've not heard of him."

Jamison replied to this effect, "Murphy heads a group of murderers and thieves commonly referred to as the *Gang of Twenty*. They operate in the northern part of the Colorado as well as parts of the Wyoming and Montana Territories. He has been the scourge of miners and cattlemen, not to mention stagecoach and rail entities for the past two years. The judge set his sights long ago to bring that man to justice. Now he is within our reach."

Presently we arrived outside of Ma Sterling's boarding house. It was a two-story frame building near the city center in a residential district. A white picket fence surrounded the house. A neatly manicured lawn added to its attractiveness. We dismounted, then tied up at the hitching rack as Jamison explained, "Ma Sterling and her late husband came to the area in the early days of the Pike's Peak gold rush of 1859. It has been said that close to a hundred thousand gold hungry adventurers swarmed into the area. In fact, Denver City developed as a mining camp during that time, eventually growing into the present city. Anyway, the Sterlings originally tried their hand at prospecting but due to a mining accident that left the old man crippled, they decided to glean their gold by other means. They chose to build this boarding house and have been quite successful with it. The judge and his wife are good friends with Ma."

We entered the gate and tramped up to the porch where a couple of wicker rocking chairs invited relaxation. Jamison opened the front door and we stepped into the hallway and removed our hats. The parlor on the left looked comfortable enough. It had a polished wooden floor with a settee and a couple of overstuffed chairs. Numerous pieces of artwork hung in groups of two and a vase of roses sat on a small table next to one window that faced the street. An old Plains rifle with power horn hung above the fireplace. Two candleholders with candles sat on either side of a portrait of Joshua Sterling on the mantel. A small table with an oil lamp stood in front of the street side window. A metal matchbox lay beside it. A writing table with paper, pen, and ink stood against the remaining wall.

I peered into the next room, which by the long table, let me know that it was the dining room. Jamison grinned at me, then shouted out, "Ma! Hey, Ma! Come on out here. I've got a new boarder for you to meet."

Momentarily, we heard a voice from the kitchen area respond, "Aw, pipe it down, Jamison! I heard you come in. Be there in a jiffy." A minute or so later a stout older woman in her fifties emerged from the kitchen. Apron-clad, with smudges of flour on her otherwise rosy cheeks, she smiled as she appraised my lanky frame.

Jamison led off with, "Ma, I'd like you to meet Cole Stockton. He was just sworn in by Judge Wilkerson and needs a decent place to call home."

Ma Sterling nodded her understanding and, with hazel eyes sparkling, held out her hand to me. "Marshal Stockton, I am Ellen Sterling. Most people just call me Ma. I run a clean house, do your laundry, and provide good food for my boarders. I don't cotton to those that over indulge in gambling, spirits, or other such nonsense. I suppose that the judge wants you to have the usual agreement. Well, for all that I provide, the monthly fee is fifteen dollars." Then, she added with a sly grin, "Payable in advance."

Jamison chuckled a bit while I rummaged in my jeans pocket to come up with a twenty-dollar gold piece. She reached into her apron pocket and came up with a wad of bills. Ma counted out five dollars in currency and handed them to me. The gold coin went into her pocket. "Follow me," she motioned, as she led us down the hall to my room. Jamison was quartered right across the hall.

4

The room was spacious enough. A small potbellied stove stood in a corner. A single window was adorned with broadcloth green curtains. The bed looked comfortable. It held a down pillow along with two wool blankets. A small chest of drawers with mirror stood along the entrance wall and on it sat a porcelain basin with pitcher for water, homemade soap, and washrag. A large towel lay across the foot of the bed. A cedar clothes closet stood at the foot of the bunk. Overall, it was a great room to call home.

Jamison picked up the conversation, "And best of all, Cole, there's a stable and corral out back for our horses as well. Let's get them put up. I imagine that you would like to take a bath and get cleaned up. The washroom is at the front of the hall."

Ma joined in, "Yes, I like my guests to wash up for supper, which reminds me, supper is served promptly at six o'clock sharp, whether you are here or not. Coffee is on with first light, and breakfast is served at six each morning. I do have a lunch available around noon, if you are in town. Feel free to share the daily *Rocky Mountain News*, our local newspaper, with other guests. Well, got to get back to fixing supper." With that, Ma went about her kitchen duties.

Jamison and I stabled the horses. He had some business to attend. It seems that until suppertime I was left to my own devices. The mention of cleaning up sounded good. So, with a change of clothes, my shaving mug, and razor in hand, I tramped down the hall. Ma Sterling had seen to it that the galvanized tub contained warm water, so I shucked my sweat-stained traveling clothes and immersed myself into the first full bath since beyond my remembrance.

*   *   *

Morning brought the aroma of fresh coffee brewing. Rising slowly, I gazed around the room. A glance to the window brought the realization that the sun had not yet come over the horizon. I thought seriously about returning to slumber when the nearby greeting of a rooster announced the new day. I exhaled a long sigh and eased up in bed.

Within the next few minutes darkness transitioned to a light gray before the first rays of warmth slowly brought life to the city. I rose and began to dress, my eyes settling on the U.S. Deputy Marshal's star. I picked it up and fingered it for a few moments reflecting on the oath that I had taken. The *Star* was only a symbol, but within me came the realization that I had committed myself and my honor to serving out justice amongst the hardships that I would endure. The trails that I would follow and the men that I would either kill or bring to court were paramount to the challenges. I wondered then if I were truly good enough to wear it. Time would tell. I pinned the six-pointed symbol of justice to my shirtfront and stepped out to meet the day.

Ma Sterling was quite pleasant when I lumbered to the kitchen and peeked in. The aroma of a fine breakfast filled the room. "Help yourself to coffee, there's cups aplenty on the sideboard," she advised. Two other young apron-clad women were with her, frying thick sliced bacon, retrieving biscuits from the oven, and arranging serving platters with flapjacks, fried eggs, and potatoes. A large tureen of corn meal mush sat to the side. Ma Sterling's idea of a good breakfast meal surely met mine.

Within minutes other boarders arrived in the dining room. I exchanged pleasantries with two young ladies as they seated themselves. I learned that one was a schoolteacher and the other owned a millenary. Both seemed interested in my newly acquired symbol of justice. We were shortly joined by five gents, one of whom was George Jamison. He broke the silence with, "Good morning, Cole. I trust you slept well because we have a good ride ahead of us this morn," before he introduced the male boarders. A couple of them were interesting fellows.

One man was employed with the express office as assayer. His job was to determine the pureness of gold or other minerals submitted for value. Another boarder told of his employment as a surveyor. One solidly-built gent who sported a fancy two-gun rig, eyed me up and down before grunting an acknowledgement. I had seen his type before. He identified himself as an entrepreneur of a most dangerous profession.

George Jamison explained it with disgust on his face as—bounty hunter. The man did not like the term and scowled back at George, who just laughed him off saying, "It seems that Ollie don't like U.S. Marshals in the Territory because we've put a damper on his business. Before he can get to his quarry, we've already arrested or killed them." I observed Ollie's reaction and I could tell that he dearly wanted to accost Jamison on that point, but thought better of it.

At precisely eight o'clock, we were admitted to Judge Wilkerson who presented us with the legal papers to take charge of none other than, Frank Murphy. Jamison put the papers into the inside pocket of his coat, then asked the judge if there were any more instructions. Judge Wilkerson reflected only a moment before retorting, "I expect that Murphy will be brought to this court in one fashion or another—standing or over the saddle, and I don't care which." Jamison and I understood the judge's message.

CHAPTER TWO

Fort Collins

"Fort Collins is mainly a farming community some sixty or so miles north of Denver." explained George Jamison as we rode out of the city heading north. "Starting out in early morning on horseback will put us there in about a day and a half."

I wondered at that time what business an outlaw like Murphy would have in a town like Fort Collins. I suspected perhaps he was casing the local bank like the James and Younger boys have been known to do.

Traveling was certainly in my blood. The two of us made talk as we rode at a steady pace toward Fort Collins. Secretive as Jamison was on our first trek together, he now opened up. They say that *birds of a feather flock together* and in our case, it was certainly true. He told me about his girl in Denver. Elizabeth, he said, was a blonde-haired beauty who admired his service to the territory. She was enthralled that he was a deputy marshal. I could see by the sparkle in his eyes that he loved this woman. I wondered if I could ever in my life find a woman I could love.

Jamison spoke of meals his lady friend had prepared for him, of walks in the parks in Denver that they took, of unspoken messages eye to eye that they shared. For all of his knowledge of the wilds of the Colorado, the woman that he described to me was more a city girl than the type of woman coveted by those who braved wild trails in search of the most dangerous. I held my tongue in respect, while I conjured up a woman in my own mind that understood the dangers that I faced as well as the reputation I held—gunfighter.

At midday we stopped beside a creek, unsaddled, and ate a small lunch of ham and cheese sandwiches that Ma Sturgis had kindly fixed for us. Our horses drank of the cool water and grazed on tall grasses near the embankment. I watched the flow of the creek for a while, taking in with considerable interest, the darkened shapes darting to and fro in the water. Periodically one would rise to the surface to snatch up an unlucky insect. I got to thinking about the times Pa, Jasper Rollins, my brother Clay, and I sat on the bank of the creek back home sharing stories as we waited for the fish to bite. Those times seemed so long ago.

After an hour's rest, we saddled up and continued our ride northward. Jamison outlined our plans as we rode. He figured that we would arrive in Fort Collins around noon the following day. We would check in with Sheriff Latimer before we checked into a hotel for the night. We would be at the jail early the following day with a saddle horse and a gunnysack of supplies for the return trip.

If all went well, we would be back in Denver with Frank Murphy by early afternoon the following day. George went on to say that his Elizabeth and her parents would expect him for dinner that evening. He inquired if I might like to accompany him. It would be an opportunity to meet a typical Denver family, not to mention the love of his life. I agreed.

Just before sundown we reached the South Platte River, like cattle drovers we crossed to the other side before setting up camp for the night. We stripped the gear off our horses before placing saddles, blankets, and bedrolls near the small fire pit that we scooped out of the earth. Jamison hobbled his mount. I knew Chino would remain nearby. With a good fire going, we boiled water, throwing some ground coffee beans into the pot. Fireside coffee has a way of making you feel at home in the wilds. It was warm beans and biscuits with a cup of hot coffee for supper.

The following morning brought the hint of rain with a cool breeze from the northwest. Although sunlight appeared in the east, the mountains to the west were unsettled with gray clouds building. George studied the weather for a bit then commented, "Cole, I think that we can be in Fort Collins before the rain hits. Let's get mounted."

We barely made the livery at Fort Collins when the first roll of thunder crashed and lightning lit up the sky. A few minutes later the sky opened to pour rain into the dusty street, turning it to mud. I had no doubt that the farming community took a liking to it. Jamison and I donned our slickers, and with Winchesters and saddlebags in hand, slogged down the street to the one-story stone building that served as the jail.

Inside, there were two cells across the back of the building with a small office space in front. A potbellied stove stood to one side and a rifle rack hung on the opposite wall. I glanced over to the one occupied cell and my blood ran cold. Frank Murphy sat on the bunk rolling a smoke. He turned to appraise us with dark calculating eyes. A sneer crossed his lips as he listened in on the conversation.

Sheriff Latimer looked up from behind his desk. He was a portly fellow dressed more like a field hand than lawman. He wore an old Colt Model 1860 revolver converted to cartridges high on his waist letting me know that he was not a gunman. The lone deputy sipping coffee in the corner was a thinner man who looked more like a storekeeper than an officer of the law. The shotgun held across his knee, however, indicated his resolve.

"Who are you and what business do you have here?" Latimer questioned. George opened his slicker to show his Deputy U.S. Marshal Star. I did likewise. The deputy seemed to relax a bit. "We are here to escort Frank Murphy to Denver, Sheriff. We will take him off your hands tomorrow morning," advised Jamison, "How many deputies do you have to guard the jail until then?"

"There is just me and Deputy Taylor here along with two more men that I deputized for this situation," remarked Latimer. He continued, "This is a farming community and people here don't think that we need more than two lawmen to keep the peace."

I spoke up, "Sheriff, I'm curious. Just how did you capture Murphy?" Sheriff Latimer related, "The Wells Fargo express agent recognized Frank Murphy from a wanted poster when he stopped in to check the stagecoach schedule. The agent then pulled a hidden pistol from under the counter and held Murphy at bay while sending a customer for the law. He surrendered peaceably enough. We've held him here for the past three days."

Jamison and I looked at each other for a moment. I could tell he was thinking the same as me, that Murphy was in town casing it for a robbery at some point. Once his followers missed him, they would be checking to determine his whereabouts.

Breathless, a young man from the telegraph office entered the jail. "Sheriff," he reported, "the wire is dead between here and

Cheyenne. Denver does not respond either. Lightning must have struck the line somewhere as it moved through the area. It will be tomorrow morning before we can get crews to ride the line and repair it."

Frank Murphy sneered a crooked smile at the news as he leaned back on the bunk, cigarette smoke drifting lazily around his head.

My thought was, "Lightning possibly, but more likely, someone doesn't want urgent news to get outside Fort Collins." I expressed that thought in low tones to Jamison and he nodded his agreement.

Turning to Latimer, Jamison expressed, "Sheriff, Marshal Stockton and I are going to grab a quick meal at that café across the street. We will be back after that and talk more. In the meantime, I would lock the front door and challenge anyone who knocks. That telegraph may have been hit by lightning, but let's not take any chances." We turned and stepped out to the street, closing the heavy wooden door behind us.

Glancing up and down the street, I observed five riders swing into the livery area as the steel bolt slid into lock position behind us. The rain was now a light mist as we cautiously made our way through the mud to the café. We took a window seat.

Dusk moved in while we ate. I felt a bit uneasy and could not pinpoint why. Something nagged in the back of my mind and it would not let go. Those five riders at the livery! That was it! I peered out to an empty street. I pondered the why of five riders resembling drovers when this was farm country. It just didn't add up.

Suddenly, a loud explosion shook the café windows. I glanced out to see smoke billowing from the rear of the jail. Jamison and I jumped up drawing revolvers as we made eye contact. We both hit the door scrambling into the muddy street.

Fortunately, we held our footing and as we rounded the rear of the jail, Murphy was attempting to mount a very skittish horse. Three men were already mounted with pistols in their hands. Two more were sloshing in mud amongst milling animals while trying to pull themselves into saddles.

Jamison and I both fired at the same instant with smoke and hot lead blossoming from our Colts. My man jerked violently out of the saddle, splashing into the mud. He never moved again. Jamison's man pitched backward to the ground, his empty eyes staring into the overcast sky.

Bullets smacked into the stone wall behind us. I returned fire as I ran up to Murphy and tried to grab him. He fought me off, holding on to the reins of his mount with one hand while wildly swinging at me with the other. I side-stepped him, swinging the barrel of my Colt across the bridge of his nose. He staggered backward, blood spattering across his face before falling into the mud. His intended mount broke loose and galloped off into the night, following the remaining outlaws that fled for safety.

Jamison fired a few rounds toward the riders, hitting one who slumped forward in the saddle, but held on. I stepped up to Murphy, Colt ready for action. He held his broken nose with his left hand. "Oh Jesus!" he exclaimed, looking up at me with venomous eyes.

A moment later, a dazed sheriff limped hurriedly around the corner of the jail to stare into the bore of Jamison's Colt. "Damn, Latimer, don't ever come up behind a man like that," spat George as he holstered his weapon. "Where is your deputy?"

Latimer had to clear his mind for a moment before replying, "Out cold on the floor. He must've got hit with a flying rock."

Together, Jamison and I picked up Murphy from the mud and walked him back into the jailhouse. Townspeople appeared on the boardwalks trying to understand what had happened. A second off-duty deputy came running up the street, gun in hand with shirttails flapping.

Inside the jail, Deputy Taylor lay sprawled with blood at the back of his head. Rocks of various sizes lay over the floor inside and outside the damaged cell. I locked up Murphy in the second cell, which miraculously stood intact, while Latimer and Jamison checked the fallen lawman. "He's unconscious but alive," mouthed Jamison.

Seconds later, a doctor appeared in the doorway with his black bag. He immediately attended Miller. From inside the cell, Murphy grumbled, "Hey! What about me? I'm still bleeding."

I looked at George Jamison, "Well, he didn't escape this time, but I'll be surprised if they don't try again before we get him to Denver."

Jamison agreed, "Yes, we'll have to be careful. I don't think that they'll try anything else tonight. Let me think ahead to our return route. Maybe I can pinpoint possible ambush sites. I think it best that one of us remain here at the jail tonight. I will take the first watch. Cole, you relieve me at three in the morning."

I nodded my concurrence and as I stepped through the door, I met a man dressed in black. He inquired, "I heard the gunfire. Are my services needed?"

He was the undertaker. "Not inside," I remarked as I pointed to the rear of the building. "There are two out back that do." Brushing past him, I went back across the street to pay for our meal. After that, I went to the one place where I figured to get a few hours sleep—the livery.

* * *

Curious bystanders gathered in small groups along the main street early the next morning. I could see a few others watching intently through the window as they breakfasted in the café. George Jamison came up the street with three saddled horses and hitched them in front of the jail.

I rousted Murphy out and handcuffed his hands in front of him. Except for a black eye and patch of bandage over his nose, he looked none-the-worse for wear. Deputy Taylor had been hospitalized with a concussion. Citizen Deputy, Ed Carmichael, and a limping Sheriff Latimer accompanied us to the street where I aided Murphy in mounting his animal.

Once mounted, Deputy Marshal Jamison led out toward the Cherokee Trail, the main stagecoach road to Denver. Chino and I trailed behind Murphy, eyes ever vigilant on the surrounding terrain.

We had traveled about twelve miles when we met up with a cavalry squad partaking of their noonday meal. The coffee smelled good and I said so to the sergeant in charge. They were kind enough to share a cup with us along with a bit of beans, bacon, and hard biscuits. Since they were headed in our direction, we rode along with them for a few miles. Murphy did not like that one bit. Periodically, I caught him sneaking a peek over our back trail.

Near to dusk, we approached the Waneka Stagecoach Station. Jamison related that the stationmaster and his wife provided good meals and a resting place for coach passengers as well as other travelers. We approached slowly, taking note of the activity. Nothing seemed out of the ordinary. Hostlers were busy pitching hay for the corralled horses, a few men and women sat in wicker chairs to take in the sunset. Two men sat at one end of the porch smoking homemade cigarettes while they sipped coffee.

We rode up to the stable area and dismounted stiffly. I stomped around a bit to get circulation back into my legs, then helped Murphy dismount. Jamison led our animals into the stable and stripped the gear off them. I gave Murphy the job of rubbing down his horse with an old potato sack. He did rather well considering I refused to un-cuff him. After washing up out back, we entered the stationhouse to the aroma of a fine venison stew and freshly baked bread.

We took our places at the far end of a long wooden table where I dished up Murphy's plate and cut his meat for him. He was surly and agitated over having to eat with his wrists shackled. Later, I found a place for him near the fireplace, shackling one wrist to a large heavy wooden chair. I figured that he could rest a bit, but still be secured. Jamison and I took turns sitting up with him while the other travelers went upstairs to more comfortable quarters.

The station came alive just before sun-up with the stationmaster and his wife firing up the kitchen woodstove. The aroma of fresh ground coffee lingered in the air as I waited for the first cup of the day. The stationmaster unbarred the front door of the building and stepped out into the cool morning air. He hesitated briefly while he stretched out his arms and inhaled deeply.

Murphy was awake, so I un-cuffed him from the chair. He rose to his full height, "I want to wash up a bit before breakfast, Marshal." I nodded and motioned him to precede me out the door. I grabbed up my Winchester as I passed it and, close behind him, we walked around the building to a washstand. He filled the basin and began to wash his face.

Suddenly, I sensed a rush of feet and turned to find two men running toward me with revolvers drawn. Murphy turned on me, swinging the cuffs. That's when I clubbed him on the side of his head with the butt of the rifle and, turning quickly back, levered rounds into the chamber and shot both men through the body at close range.

Seconds later, a bullet whined past my head and smacked into the stone structure. I traced the puff of smoke, then fired rapidly to both sides of it. Someone screamed in pain. Jamison and the stationmaster piled out of the house with rifles at the ready. No more firing came. George Jamison took charge of Murphy who now had a swollen face besides the broken nose and black eye from our previous fracas.

I cautiously advanced to whence the shot came from, carefully working my way through the heavy brush. I found where one man had been hit, splotches of blood on the ground with a trail of drops leading to a gully where horses once stood. The bushwhacker had mounted and ridden away.

When I returned to the stationhouse, Murphy was holding a wet rag to his head with once again handcuffed hands. He stared daggers at me. I looked into his battered face saying, "Murphy, you must like pain. You try that again, I'll shoot you." That gave him something to think about.

A few hours later, we were again on the trail to Denver. It looked to be a clear road when a dozen or so riders appeared a short distance behind us. I yelled out to Jamison who looked back and motioned for us to spur our mounts. Murphy looked back and grinned at me, trying to rein in his animal. I rode up beside him and jabbed spur to his horse's flank. It surged ahead. Our mounts stretched out in a ground-eating run.

Within moments bullets whined through the air. Suddenly, Jamison lurched back in the saddle and then flopped forward against his mount's neck. He hung on, still spurring his mount and whipping the reins to and fro. Murphy spurred his horse to ride side by side with Jamison.

In an act of complete desperation, guiding his mount with his legs, Murphy reached over with cuffed wrists and jerked Jamison's revolver from his holster. He fumbled with the gun while trying to regain control of the reins. He succeeded, then jerked back tightly on the reins. His horse broke stride, faltering.

Murphy turned in the saddle and before he could level the pistol at me, a bullet took him through the body. He jerked upright and another hit him. He slipped to the right as his horse stumbled and went down with him rolling over the man's right leg. Jamison also tumbled from his horse to the ground and rolled over clutching his side.

I reined in quickly, drawing my Winchester as I dismounted. I spoke to Chino, "Come on, Boy, we have done this many times before." I coaxed Chino to the ground, kneeling behind him. I levered round after round into the oncoming group. One by one I shot hell out of the men, until the remaining six gathered up a couple of wounded, veered off, and scattered back into the cloud of hanging dust. Somehow, I knew they weren't coming back. Only then did I look to Jamison and Murphy.

Jamison was badly wounded, shot twice in the back. Murphy was alive, but his right leg crushed by the animal's weight. I looked to his horse and found that it broke a foreleg when it went down. I shot it in the head, to end its misery and pulled Murphy from under it. He wasn't going anywhere, so I dragged Jamison to Murphy's dead horse, propped him up and put his revolver in his hand. "I'll be back in a few minutes," I assured both as I mounted Chino and chased down Jamison's mount. Luckily, he had not run but a few hundred yards before stopping to graze on tall grass.

Now, there was problem. I had to somehow rig two travois to carry the both of them onward, unless I could get Jamison mounted and rig one travois to carry Murphy. I went to some bushes off the trail and, with my sheath knife, labored until I cut some lengths of thick brush on top of which I laid our slickers and tied the arms in a knot around them. They seemed sturdy enough.

Next, I took the lariat from Jamison's horse and tied the drag securely to his saddle. I dragged a screaming Murphy to the makeshift contraption and jockeyed him to the center of it, tying him securely. He looked up at me with pain-wracked eyes, tears streaming down his dirty sweat-stained face, "You did it! You shot me, you SOB!"

I denied it, "Murphy, I didn't shoot you. Your own men shot you. I get the feeling that this time they did not want to take you from us. You are finished as their leader. They wanted to kill you so you couldn't tell on them. Churn that over in your mind for a while."

I helped Jamison into his saddle and, with my own lariat, tied him there. Then, I mounted Chino and very slowly led us forward, Murphy trying his damnedest to hold back cries of pain. "Get me to that judge," he loudly groaned through gritted teeth. "I'll get them sonofabitches. I'll tell everything. I'll give names, hideouts—just get me to that judge."

An hour or so later, I waved down an approaching ranch couple in a wagon and had them turn the wagon around. The man helped me get Murphy and Jamison into the wagon bed and we drove the rest of the way to the Denver Territorial Jail. Guards carried Murphy to a hospital room where a surgeon was summoned to operate. Jamison was also carried to a doctor. After delivering our prisoner to the jail, I went to see Judge Wilkerson. I related the events of the past week.

"Marshal Stockton," he began, "I told you when we met that I needed good men to help clean up this territory. I tell you now that I was right selecting you to wear *the Star*. You are a man of justice."

CHAPTER THREE

Young Laura Born To Ride

Some years earlier, in the spring of 1849, newlyweds Carroll and Mary Sumner arrived in the young and fledgling Dallas, Texas area. Like others in the Eastern states, they had heard stories of good land and opportunity in Texas and decided to make the trek. After all, the land east of the Mississippi was mostly taken by those before them and they did not have sufficient money to purchase an Eastern farm. They struck out for Texas in a wagon drawn by four horses filled with their meager possessions. Carroll drove a small herd of cattle and Mary drove the wagon.

The Trinity River area proved good soil for farming and sufficient water for irrigation. Game was also plentiful in the form of buffalo, deer, bear, turkey, and jackrabbits. The nearby creeks provided a bounty of fish. Upon arrival they were able to secure a homestead along a creek. It was enough to provide their needs.

Carroll and Mary worked the land with an innate love of nature. They held a sense of pride and accomplishment in the fall when they harvested their own crops of corn, wheat, and cotton enough for home use. Mary had a small garden of beans, tomatoes, white potatoes, sweet potatoes, squash, and carrots. Their hens provided eggs and an occasional chicken dinner.

It was also during their first harvest time that Mary knew that she was with child. The young couple reveled in that thought. At times during the term, they would sit quietly and speak of times to come, what to name their baby, what the child would be like, and things they would do together as a family.

Carroll thought like a man, "My son will grow to be strong, and love the land. He will help with the spring planting and the fall harvesting. I will pass this land on to him when the time comes."

Mary, on the other hand, thought like a woman, "I know that Carroll would love to have a son, but I should like to have a daughter. I would teach her how to cook, sew, and keep a fine home for her husband-to-be. She will be a beautiful child, and a beautiful woman. Just wait and see."

In mid-summer, Carroll summoned a neighboring mid-wife. At sunrise, a healthy dark-haired, blue-eyed little girl was born. They named her Laura Lynne.

Laura grew up learning to love the land. She asked for her own plot at age eight to grow a little vegetable garden. She learned to cultivate, work the soil, plant the seedlings, and care for the plants while the fruits of the vine matured into fresh vegetables for the table.

Laura also learned how to cook. She watched her mother as she carefully prepared various meats by searing to seal in the flavor, and then to simmer at low heat in order to allow natural juices to tenderize the selected cuts. Baking became one of her favorite pastimes. Her biscuits usually turned out flaky and savory, and her pies won compliments as most delicious. Laura learned to keep house, sew, and do all those housekeeping tasks that young women were supposed to learn. Yes, she would be an excellent wife and mother.

Laura was going on thirteen when her father's adventurous older brother, Uncle Jesse, came to visit. Jesse was a wild *mustanger* from up along the New Mexico and Lower Colorado mountain valley. Laura learned that a *mustanger* was someone who hunted and captured wild horses and broke them to saddle.

Laura was fascinated with his stories of hunting wild horses, wrangling them, and taming them, before selling them to the Army, or whomever would pay the best price.

Her Uncle Jesse boasted, "There ain't nothing twix you and God, but the wilds, and your own self. There are Indians, critters, buffalo, snakes, the elements of nature, and some mighty rough and tumble men of dubious character. A body has to carry a shooting iron all of the time, so's you can protect yourself against those that would do you harm—and there's a plenty. Some day, I hope to see some law in that territory. It would take a good man to make it stick, though, and most of those who would make a good lawman are those that are *born to the gun*. To tell the truth, I ain't seen anyone yet that I would trust to be a decent lawman up there. One day, though, there will come a man or men that will read the law of the land to those spoilers. Then and only then, the country will be a place to grow a family. You can bet your bottom dollar on it."

Uncle Jesse looked thoughtfully at Laura and asked, "Say, Laura, have you ever rode a horse—I mean, a *real horse*, not none of these here genteel farm animals, but a real, down to earth, honest to goodness, spirited horse?"

Laura confessed that "No," she indeed had never ridden anything such as her uncle had described.

"Well, Laura, dear, I've known many a horse wrangler in my day, some of the best, and you appear to have the makings of a real *horsewoman*. You have a soft voice, are tall enough, have strong hands, and I think that you have the determination to get the job done."

Laura flushed slightly at his compliment, but it planted a seed in the back of her mind. The more she thought about it, the more she wanted to be like her uncle's description of a real *horsewoman*.

She made up her mind to do so, and from that day forth, she quietly studied horses whenever she could. Laura watched them in the fields. She watched how they walked, how they ran, how they ate grass, and how they reacted in various situations.

Laura eventually realized that she was learning that each horse had its own mannerisms, but yet, all horses had common traits.

Independence Day that year brought celebrations and, of course, a rodeo. Laura looked forward with great anticipation to watching the cowboys ride the wild horses in competition.

She visited the holding pens of the wild stock the day before the celebration. She was fascinated at the variety of mannerisms of wild horses, compared to the docile animals on her parents' small farm and in those of the surrounding community.

She grew excited. She wanted to try firsthand her innate ability to handle horses. When no one was looking, she crawled under the corral bars and stood inside with the wild stock. She spoke soothingly to the collection of ten or twelve animals that stood nervously watching her—their ears pricked up and all turning to watch her every move.

Laura swallowed hard, yet walked slowly among them. This took nerve, and she wondered if she was good enough.

As the horses milled about, she felt the swelling urge to bolt screaming to the corral bars to get out as fast as possible. She fought it down. Standing perfectly still, she spoke softly to the bunch. She reached out to touch one, a mouse-colored gray, softly stroking its sleek neck. The horse stood stationary, enjoying her touch.

For a long moment, Laura sensed a spiritual attachment to the horse until her meditation was suddenly shattered with a booming voice that rang through her ears, "Hey! Hey! You! Girl! Get out of there. You could get hurt."

Laura turned to face two of the horse wranglers who had suddenly seen her in the corral. One of them was the middle-aged man who yelled at her. The younger one smiled and chuckled to himself. He thought, "A girl who knows horses. What is this world coming to?"

The older of the two was gruff and told her to stay away from the show stock. The younger man stood around six-foot. He had dark hair and eyes with a solidly-built frame. His smile told Laura that he was intrigued with her interest in the wild stock.

He introduced himself, "Hello, I'm Bill Weston. That sure took nerve. I'll bet that you would like to watch us ride, probably even learn how to ride yourself. I'd be glad to teach you a bit about riding the wild ones."

Laura was immediately infatuated with her newly found friend, yet didn't notice the sly grin on his face as he looked her over. She only looked forward to learning the trade with him. They made a pact to meet behind the corrals a few days hence and he would give her a lesson.

Two days later the rodeo was over, and most of the show was moving on. Laura met with Weston behind the corrals where he had one of the *wild* mustangs blindfolded, saddled, and ready for her.

Bill talked her through the ride that she would make, explaining how to mount, sit in the saddle, and make ready for a somewhat jolting ride. He also advised her how to dismount after several seconds. Then, he helped Laura up on the dun and waited until she was situated.

Laura took a deep breath with closed eyes for a long moment, then opened her eyes and nodded to Weston. He reached up to the bandana around the horse's face and pulled the blind off. The horse suddenly bunched up its muscles and in the next second the animal unwound like a sprung watch spring. Laura was *riding high.*

She lasted only a few seconds before flying off to land on her backside, but the experience was exhilarating. She wanted to learn more.

Bill Weston grinned with the thought, "A wild mustang girl. She needs to be tamed like the horse that she is riding, and I'm just the one to do it."

He grabbed Laura suddenly and roughly. "Come here, Mustang Girl. Here's your next lesson."

He kissed her hard on the mouth, and she fought to get away from him. Finally, she stomped down hard on his instep. Weston let go momentarily, only to grab her again roughly and wrestle her to the ground. Laura screamed loudly and the wrangler stopped in mid movement.

Voices! Someone was coming. Weston released Laura suddenly and strode rapidly to the horse. He lifted the saddle a bit, and removed the burr that he had placed there to *wild* the animal for Laura's ride. He swung quickly up into the saddle, sunk spur to the animal, and galloped out of town before anyone could see which way he went. Bill Weston was never seen in Dallas again.

A half dozen people came running to the corral to help Laura up from the ground. Her clothes were dirty and disheveled, and she had tears in her eyes. She had trusted this man, and believed in him. She had just experienced her first lesson in learning to read men.

CHAPTER FOUR

The Dark Clouds Of War

In the days that followed, talk of the Southern states seceding from the Union became the topic of conversation wherever folks gathered. In mid-April word came that rebellious troops in South Carolina had formed to fire upon Fort Sumter. The Civil War had begun.

There was uncertainty throughout Texas concerning secession. Governor Sam Houston fought against it, yet the majority of citizens were adamant. Texas seceded. Sam Houston refused to take an oath of allegiance to the Confederacy and was subsequently forced out of office. Lieutenant Governor Edward Clark then became Governor.

In Dallas County where the Sumner family lived, the citizenry overwhelmingly voted for secession. Texas would eventually enact conscription of all men from the age of eighteen to forty-eight to fill the ranks of their armies. Ten companies would be raised within Dallas County for the Confederacy with 13,000 men serving.

Because of age and marital status, Carroll Sumner was not immediately called to join one of the Texas infantry companies forming in Dallas until the later years of the war. Within a month of his conscription notice, his company would march out to an unnamed destination.

Carroll continued to farm his land until he left home. Periodically, a company of Confederate soldiers with wagons would stop by farms in the area. Under the pretense of "supporting the cause," they commandeered produce to feed the beleaguered legions staving off the impending Union horde which some anticipated to invade their beloved Texas.

One day in autumn, just after harvest, Carroll Sumner watched as two wagons escorted by five uniformed Southern cavalry soldiers entered his farmyard. The sergeant in charge rode up to Carroll and announced, "We are here to collect all you can spare for our cause."

Carroll scrutinized the sergeant as well as his followers. Something seemed amiss but he could not put his finger on it. He felt uneasy as he led the men to the corncrib where he stored harvests from the main field as well as the harvest from Mary's home garden.

Bins were stocked high with corn, potatoes, sweet potatoes, and various squash. In one section, sheaves of wheat awaited transport to the gristmill. The men backed the first wagon to the entrance and began loading it with his stores. Farm products likened to cash money in the waning days of the Confederacy.

Presently, Mary and Laura stepped out of the house to hang laundry. Carroll caught the reflection of lust in one man's eyes. Instantly, he searched the uniforms of those in the group. There were mixed insignia of various regiments. He quickly realized that these men were not regular army forces. They were scavengers—deserters who formed bands of unscrupulous men who raped, pillaged, and plundered whatever they wanted.

Carroll felt fear rising in his throat and attempted to quell it. He turned to the sergeant, "I need to write up the inventory of your acquisition. Let me get pen and paper." Carroll's choice of words took the untrained leader by surprise, but he nodded his approval while ogling Mary and the still blossoming figure of Laura from afar.

Carroll tried to walk casually to the house as "Oh God! Oh God!" surged through his mind. He couldn't hold it in any longer. Almost to his wife and daughter, he suddenly burst into a run, calling out, "Mary! Laura! Get into the house! Get the guns!" He followed them and threw the heavy bar over the latch.

Heavy bullets slammed into the door and through windows as the Sumner family readied weapons for defense. Methodically they closed shutters at every window. Each shutter was designed with a firing slit for defense against marauding Indians. Now, they would be used to defend against a different enemy, one born of lust and greed—spoilers who preyed upon remote farms in outlying communities.

Of the four weapons available to the Sumner family, Mary and Laura each took up shotguns. Carroll shoved an 1849 Walker Colt into his belt before reaching over the mantel to take down an 1855 percussion rifle, then loaded it. Carroll and Mary covered the front of their home while Laura covered the back. Carroll peered through the shutters on his side of the house. The raiders had taken cover in various places around the yard. The battle began.

Fifty caliber balls sailed into the shutters in an effort to splinter them. Bullets smacked around the door and windowsills. When one raider fired, a Sumner would return the shot. Hour after hour the Sumners held their ground until finally in the third hour the perpetrators made preparations to burn them out.

One of the farm wagons was doused with coal oil and set ablaze. Four men hid behind it as they labored to push the wagon to the front door of the house. For the Sumners the critical moment had arrived. Carroll wracked his mind trying to think of a way out of this situation. He could not. Talking hastily with Mary and Laura, they decided to fight to the last. They stood surrounding the door with weapons ready, knowing that the door would burst into flames soon.

Mary Sumner prayed silently for a miracle. It came in the form of a company of Confederate cavalry accompanied by a neighboring farmer who had heard the gunfire and witnessed the commotion. After viewing the fight undetected by the scavengers, Joshua Reynolds mounted his mule and hastened toward Dallas in search of help. He encountered Captain Goddard leading his men in search of deserters. Reynolds led them to the Sumner farm, where the troopers moved into battle line and charged into the fray.

The deserters panicked, splitting up, running in various directions across the fields into the woods. Captain Goddard's men chased them down and either shot or captured each one. Of the seven scavengers, only four were taken alive. The sergeant perished.

Hearing the volley outside, Carroll chanced a look through the shutters, and recognizing their rescuers, he exuberantly announced to his wife and daughter, "Thank the Lord, we are saved."

When the firing moved off, Carroll unbarred the door and stepped out to greet his neighbor Joshua as he dismounted. "Is anyone hurt?" inquired Joshua.

"All is well, my friend, thanks to you," replied Carroll as Mary and Laura joined them. Together they watched the remnants of the flaming wagon disintegrate in a shower of hot metal and fiery ashes.

What a blessing that the deserters had not used the wagon they loaded produce in for market in each week.

Across the field prisoners marched with hands on top of their heads, prompted by somber-faced troopers. Captain Goddard rode into the Sumner yard to convey his regrets that they "had to endure such travesty by the likes of deserter scum."

Carroll spoke for his family, "Thank you, Captain, for hastening to our rescue. Please relate our gratitude to your men as well." Goddard snapped a salute, then turned and rode to his men who prodded the captives down the road toward Dallas.

*   *   *

The following spring, Carroll Sumner hitched up his mules to plow the large field in preparation for planting his annual crop of corn. Mary dug up her garden plot and readied it for planting the family vegetable supply. Laura did likewise. Once the fields were ready the three walked the large field sowing corn and a small section of wheat. Mary and Laura planted beans, tomatoes, squash, and pumpkin. May brought the annual welcome rains that nurtured their planting.

The month of June brought Carroll's conscription notice with a report for muster date. Supper that evening included conversation regarding the war and the Dallas city muster. Carroll outlined the chores that Mary and Laura would absolutely have to perform in addition to their own in order to keep the farm running. Each held anxious thoughts about what the future would bring.

After supper, they sat on the front porch and talked of good times. Carroll read his favorite verses of comfort from the family Bible. No mention of what might come entered their conversation. Once Laura went to bed, Carroll and Mary sat together in front of their home holding hands and speaking softly to one another.

Mary cupped Carroll's face in her hands. "I have always been proud to call you my husband," she whispered softly, "know that my heart goes with you in the morrow. I will write often to keep you informed." Carroll put his arm around her, "Mary, you honor me with your love. I could ask nothing more than what you have given me. I cherish the time we have together and take pride in knowing that you are my wife. I shall also write to you as often as I can. I am justly proud of both you and our daughter."

Laura spent a fitful night for a fourteen-year-old, conjuring up visions of dark shadows engaged in deadly combat, of wounded men wracked in pain calling out for assistance. Finally, in the post midnight hours her mind was merciful as sleep overcame her fears.

*   *   *

It was the day of departure for Carroll Sumner's Dallas county infantry company. Throngs of people—mostly women, children, and older men—mingled with their loved ones to bid farewell to the complement of soldiers as they formed and prepared to march.

Laura took notice of the crowd gathered in the city square. Of particular note were the disabled veterans looking on at the proceedings. There were those missing arms and legs, there were those who had been blinded, there were those who were disfigured. She trembled with the notion that her father was embarking on the same mission given these unfortunate men.

Laura also encountered friends. One in particular, Alice Kincaid, caught her eye. Alice was beaming in excitement, her father and a brother now of age, were conscripted and marching with the company. "How grand they look," Alice exclaimed. "Aren't you proud of your father?" Laura only nodded. In the back of her mind was another thought, "Alice, you live in dreamland. Look around you. Look at those men that have fought before, think of dreams that will not be realized, think of the spoiled lives of those men. Alice, think of what might befall your loved ones." With those thoughts, Laura stood close to her father and touched his hand.

Moments later, Carroll held both of his dear ones in his arms as they hugged and spoke encouragement to one another. "Laura, dear," whispered Carroll to his daughter, as he fought back the mist in his eyes, "you will have to help your mother maintain the farm. Be brave, I know you will. In time, we will be together as a family again, I feel it in my heart. Never forget that I love you." Laura forced a smile and nodded her understanding. Carroll then turned to Mary to hold her close as he whispered his undying love in her ear.

Then, the companies formed amid choked cheers and misting eyes. The column was called, "Attention, Forward—March!" Led by fife and drum, the company stepped gallantly forward through the dusty streets of Dallas toward their destination and their destiny.

Mary and Laura Sumner watched with heavy hearts as the column slowly faded from view. Each turned to look into one another's eyes with mounting concern for Carroll's well being. They hugged in an effort to quell the fear that quivered within them. The ladies would work the farm without Carroll to maintain their land until this terrible strife was over. They would begin their first letters to Carroll that very evening after chores.

Weeks passed before the women received the first letter from Carroll. Prior to that word, Mary and Laura anxiously awaited copies of the weekly newspaper, the *Dallas Herald*, in order to scan the dreaded casualty lists with hearts pounding. Each week they breathed sighs of relief when Carroll's name did not appear.

*   *   *

Carroll Sumner marched away with mixed feelings. His heart was heavy with concern, not for himself, but for his beloved wife and daughter. With him were his friends and neighbors. Most had voted for secession. With Federal victories throughout the South, the men of Dallas joined the Confederate effort to turn the tide of the ever-advancing blue clad thunder.

Several days into the march, the company joined other Confederate forces under the command of General John B. Magruder, Commander of the District of Texas. When the terrain turned more wooded, it prompted a soldier to comment to Carroll, "I don't believe that we are in Texas anymore." The next evening, they camped near the East Texas town of Tyler.

As the men enjoyed coffee after supper, several wagonloads of wounded Union soldiers passed near the infantry camp as well as prisoners on foot under guard of a cavalry unit. Word around the campfire gave rumor to a prisoner camp in this area.

After their morning routine of breakfast and chores, the Company Commander called the men in Carroll's company to order. He began, "We are near Camp Ford outside Tyler. It is currently a prison for

Union soldiers taken in the Red River campaign area." He paused to collect his thoughts, then continued, "At Officer's Call this morning, I received orders to the effect that two squads of our company are detailed to serve at Camp Ford. The remaining squads will prepare to march as directed by the commanding general."

This announcement brought both cheers and adverse comments. "Listen up men!" came the stern response. "Squads two and four will assemble and march to Camp Ford at nine AM. The First Sergeant will inform each man of his detail." With those remarks, the commander disappeared into his tent.

Rumbles among the men continued. Were they expected to care for Yankee soldiers? Many of the unit were angry as they speculated that they would not see combat.

Carroll, serving in the fourth squad, was astonished to hear his assignment when his name was called out. "Carroll Sumner, report to the post surgeon at the prison hospital at one o'clock PM." He had been selected based upon recommendation of his commanding officer as a man of maturity and sound judgment. And so, it was Carroll Sumner's fate to tend the cries of the wounded as he labored as a surgeon's assistant the last year of the war.

In late April 1865, dispatches bore the fateful news. General Robert E. Lee had surrendered the Army of Northern Virginia at Appomattox Courthouse. Confusion reigned for several weeks. In mid-May the prison commander announced that the entire Texas Army was disbanded. Carroll Sumner could return home to his beloved family. Upon gathering up his meager belongings, he surveyed the Tyler-based prison unit, then along with other Dallas based soldiers, began his long walk home.

*   *   *

Mary and Laura were working in the field when a rider galloped up the road from Dallas waving a broadside in his hand and shouting to the world, "It's over! The war is over! Lee surrendered! The war is over!" Mary fell to her knees as she lifted her face to the heavens, "Thank you, Lord. May Carroll be on his way home soon." Laura stood beside her with eyes closed, imagining her father walking down the road to turn in at their farm.

29

CHAPTER FIVE

The Prediction

On her eighteenth birthday, Laura's mother held a small party in her honor at their home. One guest in attendance was an elderly lady named Maude Pritchard.

Maude was said to be *psychic.* Her intuition about most people she met was usually correct. Maude was often hired to entertain at parties. Each person attending would have a steaming cup of tea before she read fortunes by closely examining the trail of tea leaves.

Most town folk agreed that Maude was quite accurate. Those who had their fortunes read could count on the blessings or fret about the uncertain times that she foretold.

Mary Sumner took pride in introducing Maude Pritchard to her young daughter. Maude gazed into Laura's bright blue eyes for only a moment. The elderly woman smiled, then commented, "You love horses very much, don't you? I can see you with many, many horses in the future."

Laura was quite taken by that statement. Coming from a person she hardly knew, it was a most profound revelation. Laura had never mentioned to anyone that she wanted to raise horses someday.

The party went well. Everyone thoroughly enjoyed the special cake that Mary Sumner baked and decorated for the occasion. Everyone sipped tea, and one by one, the guests got to hear their fortunes told by the tea leaves. They had great fun listening to the predictions Mrs. Pritchard shared.

As a finale, Laura's fortune was read. Maude turned the teacup upside down on the saucer, rotated the cup three times, then turned it right side up again. She scrutinized the patterns of the tea. Maude looked deep into Laura's eyes, and said softly, "There will be sorrow at the loss of one close to you, but through this loss you will profit.

30

I see mountains. I see a dream fulfilled. There will be a man in your life—one who carries a heavy burden. He is a man given of deadly skill and authority. Through him you will have many adventures. There will be love."

Laura's parents, as well as, attending guests stood in silent awe as a visibly blushed Laura pondered this prediction. What did it mean? In the years that followed, she would recall hearing these profound words as her destiny unfolded.

Over the next couple of years, several young men came to call on Laura. Each was interesting and quite likeable in his own way, but every one of them was somehow not the man that Laura envisioned to be the one to make her life with. Besides—she still had her dream to fulfill.

When she celebrated her twentieth birthday, Laura decided to visit her Uncle Jesse in the lower southern Colorado valley area. She would learn the wild horse business firsthand from a man she could trust.

She discussed the journey with her parents, and within the month boarded a stagecoach to the wilds of Colorado, and her destiny.

The coach trip was long but exciting for Laura. There were many interesting passengers who traveled her way. One traveling companion, a man in a dark suit, had discretely armed himself. Whenever he leaned a certain way, she could see the butt of a pistol underneath his coat. Laura liked his hazel eyes. He had dark hair, and a trimmed mustache. This quite handsome fellow smiled frequently at her. They eventually introduced themselves to each other. His name was Brett Parsons and he was from San Antonio.

Brett enthusiastically explained that he was on his way to the New Mexico Territory to seek his fortune. His dream was to someday own a small ranch of his own, get married, and raise a family.

Laura spoke of her dream of raising horses, and the two of them shared thoughts of what it would be like raising horses on the Western frontier.

The land, they found, was rather desolate with rolling hills and cactus. The heat was stifling. Dust storms came up from nowhere, blowing for a while, and then simply died away quickly. Other irritations included periodic swarms of gnats and flies that the coach drove through. About every twenty-five or so miles, the coach would pull into a *swing station* to change teams. The passengers dismounted, walked around a bit, got a drink of water, and for a scant fifteen minutes or so relaxed before re-boarding the coach to continue onward.

As they neared Las Vegas, New Mexico, the coach suddenly lurched forward as the driver yelled to his team and cracked his whip high over the heads of the horses. Laura and Brett were quickly thrown together. He held her in his arms as their eyes searched each other. The momentary spell was broken, however, by the sharp crackling of gunfire. A bullet whined through the coach and thudded into the padded wall just under the driver's side.

Brett quickly pushed Laura down to the floor of the coach, and drew his revolver—an ivory handled .38 caliber Colt Lightning, "A holdup!" yelled Brett. "Laura, stay down on the floor. We're being chased by outlaws." Quickly, he turned to the window of the coach, steadied his arm to resist the jostling, then took aim at the gaining horsemen. Several bullets smacked into the windowsill sending splinters flying. More bullets smacked into the coach wall.

Laura lay on the bottom of the coach floor wishing that she could see what was going on, and offering a quick prayer that the coach could outrun the outlaws. She heard the shotgun guard's booming response to the whining of the holdup men's bullets.

A long fifteen-minute chase culminated in one of the coach horses taking a bullet and crumbling in the traces. The other horses tried to drag the carcass, but eventually slowed to a straining walk.

Four masked riders abruptly surrounded the stagecoach waving pistols, yelling for passengers to dismount and line up. There was nothing to do but comply. Brett dropped his revolver on the floor between the seats, then helped Laura from the coach. She glanced quickly around, taking note of the outlaws' dress and especially their horses. All four men were slovenly, their shirts stained with sweat, their hands rough and grimy. The stench of stale sweat permeated the air around them.

Three of the holdup men dismounted. Two went to work forcing the lock off the money box and the third one stepped up to Laura with an empty grain sack in his hand. "Your valuables, Missy, and don't hold nothing back. Well, now, ain't you the purty thing. Hey, boys, maybe we ought to take her with us—for protection."

The unsavory man moved to take Laura's arm but she withdrew it. He lunged a step closer to her, reaching out to grab her. Brett quickly moved to knock the man's hand away. The outlaw turned on Brett and clubbed him mercilessly about his head with his heavy handgun again and again amid Laura's screams, "Leave him alone!" The mounted outlaw stopped him with a sharp command. "That's enough! You've made your point."

Harsh words ensued between the two men. The angry fellow finally bowed to the wishes of the leader, then remounted his horse. Laura burned the look of the man into her mind. She memorized his description as well as the sound of his voice. She would remember this man. Uncle Jesse's words flashed in her mind, "A body has to carry a shooting iron all of the time, so's you can protect yourself against those that would do you harm—and there's a plenty."

The holdup foursome wheeled their mounts, and dashed off with loud, boisterous, foul-mouthed remarks. Once they were out of sight, Laura and the shotgun guard turned to Brett. He was seriously injured. Blood trickled from his mouth and ears. Laura surmised that he was dying from the pistol beating he had taken about the head.

Brett's eyes glazed over, but he held tight to Laura's arm. Words slurred as he told her to take his Colt revolver and keep it for her own protection. She promised that she would, and then he closed his eyes, sighed, and passed on.

Laura's eyes filled with tears, but a burning determination to see justice throbbed throughout her entire body. She was learning a lot about the brand of men out here in the lawless West, and now she would study men as closely as she watched horses. She would come to read men by the seemingly little things within their mannerisms and actions.

The men wrapped Brett in blankets and lifted him gently to the top of the coach where they tied him down securely. The driver cut loose the dead animal before he urged the remaining horses onward.

Laura sat alone as she thought of the men that held up the stage. Although they covered their faces with bandanas, she would always remember the wild eyes of the man who viciously killed Brett. She recalled how they dressed, how they wore their guns slung low to wrist level. She thought of other men she knew who wore guns.

Their guns were high on their waists. The difference was suddenly clear to her. A man who wears his gun belt slung closer to his wrist uses it quite frequently, and wants it in a hurry—a gunman.

The remainder of the trail to Las Vegas, New Mexico, proved uneventful. Dozing on the rear seat of the coach as they neared the town, Laura awoke with an eerie feeling. She shivered a bit, then leaned toward the window just in time to catch the blurry vision of a man on horseback loping past the coach.

The young woman glanced backward at him and watched him slow his roan to an easy walk. She saw only his back; however, the rider appeared to be tall and of slender build. He wore a dark shirt, dark hat, and light bandana. Momentarily, the coach swung into the main street of Las Vegas, and the rider was out of sight.

A crowd had gathered around the sheriff's office, directly across the street from the stage depot. Laura was helped down from the coach by the stagecoach agent. She inquired the reason for the crowd.

"Well, Miss," grunted the agent, "those two fellers laid out in front of the sheriff's office rode into town a few hours ago raising dust and shouting obscenities. One of them accosted a young townswoman as she walked past the saloon. They was told to unhand her. Together they turned to face the demand as they drew their revolvers. Low and behold, this feller they faced drew and fired three rounds. It was the fastest draw anyone in these parts ever laid eyes on. Took the big guy twice in the chest, the other straight in the gut. Both were gone for within minutes."

At that moment, the man who rode shotgun on the stage approached Laura. "Miss Sumner, there's something I think you ought to see. I need your witness to back me up, but, I believe that those two dead men laid out in front of the sheriff's office are two of the men that held up the stage and killed your friend."

Laura accompanied the guard to the front of the crowd. Propped up and tied to planks, were indeed two of the men who had stopped the coach. She identified the one who had accosted her and pistol whipped Brett to death. Two bullet holes in the center of the man's chest, spaced about an inch apart, indicated that his executioner used deadly force with pin-point accuracy. "He doesn't look so tough now," she thought.

A man wearing the badge of a Deputy United States Marshal approached the sheriff. "Sheriff Jackson, is Cole Stockton still in town? I need to speak with him."

Sheriff Jackson shook his head, "No, Marshal Jamison. You just missed him. He rode out just as the stage arrived."

Laura felt shivers once more as she looked questioningly at the sheriff, "Who is Cole Stockton?"

Sheriff Jackson turned somber-like but answered, "Well, Miss—Cole Stockton is a gunfighter, and probably the best man with a gun in these parts. He's a quiet man, normally rides alone. When provoked, is lethal—as these two can attest. There are some that would like to bury him, and there are others who wish that they had his skill with a six-gun."

A sense of loneliness settled into Laura's mind, and she didn't know why. Silently, she thanked the man who dealt justice to the outlaws. He had made an imprint on her first journey alone into this beautiful, as well as treacherous part of the country.

CHAPTER SIX

Jesse's Lessons

The trip from Las Vegas, New Mexico, to the wild Lower Colorado Territory was fairly uneventful. As the coach neared Laura's destination, the driver slapped the reins, and cracked his long whip high over the heads of the horses as he called out to his team, "Ho Sally, Ho Jocko, get up there Sammy. Lead them wheelers, Banjo!"

Laura felt the surge of the team as the coach rocked fore and aft. She was situated right behind the driver, which was the most coveted place inside the coach for comfort. She felt the excitement rising in her body. She was almost to the town nearest Uncle Jesse's ranch. She squirmed around a bit in her seat to quickly peer out the window of the coach to see shapes in the distance become buildings of the community. They were almost there.

Long minutes later, the coach passed a sign on the outskirts of the town that read *Miller's Station*. Moments later the coach slid to a halt in front of the combination stagecoach and express office. The driver leaned down from the high box and yelled out, "Miller's Station! Those traveling onward will be ready to re-board in thirty minutes."

The right hand door of the coach was quickly opened by the station agent who helped Laura down to the loading platform. She sighed a bit and then looked around the small crowd gathered around the coach. Her heart thumped wildly as a widely grinning, Uncle Jesse stepped forward, holding out his arms to her. Laura rushed to him, throwing her arms around his neck and planting a kiss on his whiskered cheek.

Jesse was excited to see her, "Laura, my dear, it's so good to see you again. You have come at a most opportune time. I have only five wranglers to work out a couple of hundred horses. There is lots to do, and we will teach you everything about horse wrangling."

36

After the hugs and greetings, Laura glanced around the town as she waited for her trunk to be unloaded from atop the coach. Miller's Station began as a small trading post along the Purgatory River and eventually transitioned into a stopping place for travelers on the mountainous route of the Santa Fe Trail. In those days, it was not a route for the faint-hearted.

Presently the town included one main street lined with false front buildings and several residences on side and parallel streets. The main street had three saloons, the combination stagecoach depot-express-assay office, a two-story hotel next door, a large general store and mercantile. There was also a livery stable and corrals, the jail, a feed and grain store with loading docks in the back, one doctor's office, two cafés, a town meeting hall, a schoolhouse, one church, and of course, the stagecoach line barn and stables. The main business of the area was cattle and horses, along with small mining operations.

Momentarily, Jesse retrieved Laura's trunk while she carried her valise. The two walked to his ranch wagon hitched in front of the hotel next door. He put her trunk in the bed of the wagon and helped her up to the seat. Once settled beside her, Jesse turned to Laura and remarked, "Are you ready for an adventure, dear?" A smiling Laura nodded that she was.

Jesse slapped reins to the two-horse team and down the road to the west they rode. An hour later, the team drove through a gate that read, *Sumner Ranch*. Laura took in the ranch yard and the panorama of the surrounding Rocky Mountains. It was just as Jesse had described it when he visited his family in Dallas.

Laura loved the countryside as well as Uncle Jesse's ranch house. A front porch ran the width of the house where two rockers greeted guests. There was room for planting a small garden of flowers on either side of the steps. Uncle Jesse thought her idea to plant flowers was splendid. "You bring beauty to this spread," he declared.

Laura blushed. She had never thought of herself as beautiful, somewhat attractive maybe, but not beautiful. Uncle Jesse smiled at her with pride and love. "This sweet young woman cares enough to leave home and family to spend time with me," he thought.

The three months that followed brought more new learning about finding, taming, training, and riding horses than Laura ever thought possible. Luckily, she was a quick study and mastered every skill that the men taught her.

True to herself, she also studied the men that she saw in the Territory. Uncle Jesse and those who worked for him all wore their guns high on their waists. They were working men. A couple of men she observed in the small town, however, wore their pistol belts a bit lower than the average citizen. Laura pointed this observation out to Uncle Jesse.

Jesse looked at Laura, thought for a moment and replied, "Laura, you're learning to read the men out here very well, and that's good. Trust your instincts, though. Sometimes a man is not what he appears to be. For instance, take that feller over there. His name's Forgy, he's one of the sheriff's deputies."

Jesse paused a moment. "Forgy seems mighty proud of that pistol he's carrying. See the notches on the handle? There are four of them. That means that he's kilt four men in gunfights. He's bragged a bit about it, and thinks that he's one of the best."

Uncle Jesse continued, "Laura, don't ever trust him when the chips are down. A good man with a gun doesn't have to brag about it. Folks will know it. Forgy claims to have shot those fellers, but no one I know can verify it. Yessir, a good man with a gun will most likely not have notches on the handle. He knows deep within hisself how many men he's kilt, and that he will have to answer to the Almighty when the time comes."

Jesse further commented, "Laura, also study a man's eyes. His mannerisms and smiles may lie, but his eyes will always tell the truth. Look deep into a man's soul, and read it. Most honest-to-goodness gunmen keep pretty much to themselves—for survival. They can read each other's thoughts, and some I know of can put the fear of death into a man just by looking deep into his eyes—to see his soul. Keep that in mind, Laura, and you will know men far more than most."

Laura Sumner spent three months with her Uncle Jesse at his horse ranch in the wilds of the Lower Colorado Territory. Her uncle passed on a wealth of information about horses, men in general, and how to use weapons.

Laura showed him the Colt Lightning that Brett Parsons gave her before he died. The old man advised her right then and there, "If you're going to carry a gun, you'd best know how to use it."

He schooled her in the art of caring for the Colt as well as loading and using it. He used his leather skills to design, and tool a holster and cartridge belt for her. The belt fit her well, and Uncle Jesse showed her how to wear it to the best advantage of a fairly smooth draw. She learned how and when to use the pistol also.

Jesse placed empty food tins on the back corral bars every evening after chores, so that day by day, they practiced until Laura became a better than average shot. "Remember," he said, "pull it when you need it, be sure of your target, take aim and do it right. A lot of men draw their weapons too fast, and miss with the first shot. You may not get a second chance."

The day arrived for Laura to return to her family in the Dallas area. Uncle Jesse drove her to town in the ranch wagon, and waited with her for the southbound coach. They had a leisurely breakfast in the town café before departure. Laura bought a newspaper, the first that she had thought about since her arrival. "I'll read it during the trip," she thought.

Ten o'clock came, and the coach loaded up. Laura threw her arms around Uncle Jesse and kissed him a fond farewell, promising to write often. "I'd like that," responded her uncle. With those farewells and tearful eyes, Laura boarded the coach for Texas and home. A half-hour later, she finally took out the newspaper and began to read.

The headline story told of a new peace and tranquility around the eastern Colorado ranching area. It seemed that there had been the makings of a range war with one large rancher heading up raids on small homesteaders, then running them off their hard-worked land in order to expand his range.

The trouble culminated one morning in an all out gunfight at the rancher's main house. The rancher, several of his hands, and a hired gunfighter named Kid Lawrence, were killed. The wounded renegades hastily left the territory, the newspaper reported. The article further recorded that one man—Cole Stockton, dealt out the six-gun justice, standing up for the homesteaders when no one else would.

Once more, Laura felt pangs of excitement; goose-bumps spread along her arms. What was it about that name? She didn't know. She hadn't even met the man. She had only twice heard of him.

Uncle Jesse's words once again flashed across her mind, "A good man with a gun doesn't have to brag about it—folks will know it." She would miss Uncle Jesse and his *words of wisdom*.

The coach lumbered and lurched with the lay of the land, and Laura Lynne Sumner turned her thoughts toward Texas and her family.

At one point during her return trip, a tense situation ensued. The stagecoach stopped at a rest station for the usual changing of teams. The passengers stretched their legs and were able to grab a quick meal of coffee and meat sandwiches.

Laura sat at a table with three other passengers while she ate the small meal. Through the open door she casually observed three men ride up to the hitching rack, dismount, and water their horses. All three wore trail clothes, and wore their gunbelts slung low. One man wore a two-gun rig with tied down holsters so they wouldn't flap or otherwise impede a quick draw.

After several minutes, the men entered the stationhouse, spurs jingling. All three were unshaven and dusty, like they had traveled a while. They were middle-aged, hard—bodied men with weathered faces. Once inside, they moved to the serving table and took coffee and a meat sandwich each before sitting together at a back table talking in barely audible tones.

Laura remembered what her Uncle Jesse had said as she found herself studying the men's eyes. The center man looked up at her, holding her gaze, and she felt as if his eyes stared right through her. They were deep, cold—piercing. An icy cold shiver ran through her body. She felt death staring her in the eye. Laura quickly averted her gaze, and the man went back to his meal. When the men finished, they rose from the table, went to their horses, mounted, and rode off.

The man seated next to Laura breathed a sigh of relief before he spoke to the other passengers, "I'm sure glad that those men are gone. The tall one was Charlie Sturgis. He's a mean one, and faster than greased lightning. You can bet that wherever they ride, there will be killing. They hire out their guns to whomever pays the highest. I saw Sturgis in action at Santa Fe. The cowboy that he shot and killed didn't have a chance."

Laura found herself speaking under her breath, "An ordinary cowboy. I wonder how he would have faired against someone with equal or better skill? Someone like—like—her mind was racing—Cole Stockton."

The man next to her heard her words, and replied instantly, "It would be something to see alright, but I heard a rumor that Sturgis was in a saloon along the New Mexico and Colorado Territory border last spring, and heard that Stockton was in town. He packed his duff and lit a shuck out of there. I hear that there is bad blood between them, and Sturgis wants no part of Stockton."

Minutes later, the coach was ready to leave. "All aboard for Texas!" came the call from the driver, and Laura along with the other passengers returned to the coach.

CHAPTER SEVEN

A Good Friend Lost

Back at home, Laura Sumner amazed her family with stories of wild mustang hunts, riding the wild ones, training them, and driving them to sale at various ranches and mining towns in the area. She filled in details that her letters home had left out. They saw a difference in her mannerism and excitement in her eyes as she related her experiences. Carroll and Mary Sumner smiled at their daughter with knowing looks. She would go back to the territory. Her calling in life was that of an honest-to-goodness horsewoman.

Within the week, Laura's parents arranged a small welcome home party in her honor. They invited several old friends as well as some newer acquaintances. Among these new friends was Jeffrey Marlowe, a tall good-looking young man with dark hair and eyes.

Jeffrey, it seems, came to the Dallas area from Virginia, liked it, and bought a small horse ranch near the Sumner farm. His plan was to raise quarter horses. Laura's parents felt confident that Laura and Jeffrey would become fast friends. True to their thinking, Laura and Jeff compared experiences and immediately developed a liking for each other.

Another guest, Maude Pritchard, looked into Laura's eyes and remarked, "You have been to the mountains, witnessed death, and have seen your destiny." Everyone knew that Maude had the gift of prophecy.

Laura was aghast with the statement, even though everyone said that Maude had the gift of prophecy. She had told no one at home about the stage holdup or Brett's death. She had not mentioned the two dead holdup men. Neither had she expressed the fact that she had stared into a known killer's eyes and felt the bone-chilling cold of a fiery soul in hell.

Maude looked at her and nodded slightly, "We could have tea tomorrow noon, at my home." Laura agreed. This woman could see Laura's life unfolding in the young woman's eyes.

Laura and Jeff spent much of the evening together locked in conversation about horses and how best to train them. When the evening came to an end, Laura saw Jeff to his horse, a beautiful cocoa colored stallion with a white diamond on his forehead. Admiring Jeffrey's horse, the two young people stood close to each other, and their gaze reflected a more-than-average interest in each other.

Momentarily, Jeffrey looked deep into Laura's clear blue eyes and with a smile, said, "Laura, I understand that there is a barn dance this coming Saturday evening. I would be honored if you would accompany me to it."

Laura smiled demurely, "I would love to attend the dance with you, Jeffrey. What time should I be ready?"

Jeffrey seemed aglow as he answered, "I shall call for you precisely at six o'clock in my humble carriage." Then, he chuckled a bit. Laura giggled. This man had a sense of humor.

The next day around twelve o'clock noon, Laura stood at Mrs. Pritchard's door. She didn't necessarily believe in Maude's purported powers, but curiosity couldn't be denied. So here she was. The elderly lady welcomed her with a warm smile as she ushered her into the kitchen where a freshly steeping pot of herbed tea filled the kitchen with an inviting aroma.

They sat at the cozy table near the window while sipping tea. Maude spoke of her many years on the Texas frontier. Her stories of the Texas fight for independence, the Alamo, the Republic and statehood fascinated Laura. This lady had witnessed several decades of history in the Lone Star State.

"I was a wild young woman in those days," mused Maude. "I broke horses for my man, helped him fight off the raiding Comanche and rustlers, and made a home for him. I see myself in you, Laura, and know that you have seen the *critter* and you long for it. Let us look at the tea leaves once again."

Maude repeated the ritual with the teacup and studied the pattern of the leaves. She thought deeply for a long moment, then looked Laura straight in the eyes and announced, "You will be infatuated with a young man of your age. He is a lusty man, and you will have to decide your destiny. There is a loneliness. There is one who will stoke the fires of your soul. He is born of a deadly skill, yet you will seek the comfort of his honor."

Laura spent the remainder of the afternoon with Mrs. Pritchard while she pondered the prediction of the tea leaves.

The following weekend found Laura Sumner dressed in her finest gown for the dance. The dress was a deep blue satin trimmed with ivory lace. It fit in such a way to enhance her figure which naturally would stir the blood of her escort Jeffrey. Her hair lay in long dark swirls around her shoulders further enhancing the sense of excitement. An ivory broach adorned a soft blue velvet ribbon at her throat. She was a picture of blooming young womanhood.

Jeffrey arrived promptly at the given time, and she could see by his face that she had chosen the right gown. He could hardly take his eyes off her.

They danced every dance together, and during the intermission, strolled in the moonlight behind the barn. Jeffrey moved her into the shadows where they stood looking into each other's eyes.

She moved into his arms, and they kissed. Laura Sumner was alive with excitement and this man wanted her. She felt that Jeffrey could bring her dream of a horse ranch to reality. She felt that this man could bring all her dreams to reality.

The next few weeks brought Laura and Jeffrey Marlowe closer. They picnicked along the river and went for early morning rides together. Laura floated on air without a care to her name. Courtship consumed her.

Two months had passed since Laura returned from the Colorado Territory when the letter addressed to Miss Laura Sumner and postmarked from the Colorado Territory arrived. The return address was that of Wilbur Yates, Attorney at Law. Anxiously, with her mother, Mary Sumner looking over her shoulder, Laura practically tore the letter open and began to read:

Dear Miss Sumner,

I regret to inform you and your family of the
untimely death of your Uncle Jesse Sumner. He
was found dead of gunshot wounds on his grazing

range. The local sheriff's office has all of the details
and of the subsequent investigation.

I now inform you that your uncle, Jesse Sumner,
left a Last Will and Testament on file with my
office a few months ago. I am now empowered
to notify you that he willed his entire ranch,
and all additional holdings, to you.

There is the matter of several back payments
due the local bank. I have acted on your behalf,
to delay foreclosure for the next six months.
The dues must be paid in full by that time or the
ranch and all holdings will revert to the local bank.

Please notify me of your intent. I remain,

Yours truly,

Wilbur Yates,
Attorney at Law
Lower Colorado Territory

Laura could not believe her tear-stained eyes. She was devastated.
Uncle Jesse was dead, killed on his own range. She slipped from her
weeping mother's embrace and ran to the stable. She must go to
Jeffrey. She needed comfort in this hour of sadness.

Laura mounted her gray horse and fairly galloped to Jeffrey's
ranch. She quickly dismounted and ran to knock on the door. With
no answer she bolted to the stable, calling as she threw open the
door, "Jeffrey! I-I-I."

Her tear-stained face froze in disbelief. Astounded at what she
saw, Laura gasped. Jeffrey stood at the entrance of the third stall, his
clothes half off as he held a disheveled young woman in his arms.

"Damn!" whinced Jeffrey loudly, and pushed the blonde-headed
girl back from him.

Laura came to her senses. She turned, slammed the stable doors
and ran to the gray. In desperation she mounted, and nearly ran over

Jeffrey as she heeled the animal into an all-out-run for home. Jeffrey called after her, but she did not make sense of his words.

Back at home, Laura entered her parents' house, rushed into her grieving father's strong arms, only to sob uncontrollably. Mary joined them in an effort to comfort Carroll on the loss of his only brother. For Laura, there had been two devastating events in one day.

It was a week before Laura made up her mind. She would go back to Colorado, and claim the inheritance Uncle Jesse left her. She would make his ranch something to be proud of. She would fulfill her dream on her own. She went to her parents to announce her intentions.

Carroll Sumner stepped to his daughter, enfolding her in his arms. He fought back the sting in his eyes as he told her, "Laura, ever since Jesse visited us years ago, I've seen the spark of adventure in your eyes. I've seen it even more within your being since you've returned from Colorado. You are a grown woman now with dreams of your own. I will miss you terribly, but I know that you have to go. Go dear, go to seek your destiny, and always remember that we love you."

Mary Sumner held her daughter to her bosom and related, "Laura, you have the spirit of adventure about you, much like your father and I had when we were first married. We wanted a life of our own, and to that end, we chose the Texas frontier. Now, that frontier has moved beyond our farm and pushed further west. Your thirst cannot be quenched without seeking and experiencing first hand, the joy of attaining your dream. We raised you to think, and to do right by yourself. You have determination to see yourself through any situation. Your father is right. Go to find your life. We are always here for you. Get a good night's sleep, dear. Tomorrow, I shall help you pack."

The next morning, Mary helped Laura pack her belongings in a small trunk and smaller valise. Laura dressed in an emerald green traveling skirt, matching jacket, and white linen blouse with amber cameo broach at the collar. Her ensemble was completed with a black felt riding hat trimmed with dark violet lace band, ostrich plume, and netting. She put her gunbelt, and Colt Lightning into the valise.

Mary and Carroll drove Laura to the stagecoach depot in the farm wagon. They sat with her while waiting for the coach to team up. Few words were exchanged, but their eyes and soft touches said it all. It was an endearing farewell to Laura.

When the coach pulled up beside the station platform, Laura turned to her parents with a forced smile upon her face. "Write often, Dear," whispered her mother tearfully when she kissed her daughter's cheek. "God speed, and keep you," said her father. Laura hugged him lightly as she kissed his weather-beaten cheek.

Laura was the last passenger to board the coach. Once inside and situated, the door was shut, and the station agent turned to the driver, telling him to "Let it rip!" The driver snapped his whip above the heads of the team, and spoke to them, urging the horses on. The coach lurched forward, and a misty-eyed Laura Lynne Sumner waved to the beloved figures who grew smaller and smaller in the distance as the lumbering stagecoach carried her on to Colorado, and her destiny.

CHAPTER EIGHT

Miller's Station

The trip from Dallas, Texas to the small town of Miller's Station just over the passes into the Colorado Territory proved uneventful for Laura. As before, the coach ground to a halt in front of the combination stagecoach and express office. The station agent was there to open the door and help her down to the loading platform.

Disembarking from the coach, Laura once again familiarized herself with the town layout, locating Lawyer Yates' office toward the west end of Main Street. She decided to book a hotel room for the night and to visit Wilbur Yates' office early in the morning. She requested that the station agent retrieve her trunk and deliver it to the hotel next door. Then, she took up her valise and stepped quickly along the boardwalk to the hotel entrance.

After she signed the hotel register, the curious clerk examined Laura's signature, then looked questioningly at her for a long moment before inquiring, "Miss Sumner, would you be related to ole Jesse Sumner?"

"Yes, I am, "replied Laura. "I'm his niece."

The clerk turned somber as he carefully chose his next words, "Ole Jesse was well liked in this town. We are very sorry about his passing. Please accept my condolences. Will you be staying long?"

Laura nodded her gratitude as she held out her hand for the key, "I have business with Lawyer Yates and that business will determine my stay." In the back of her mind, Laura thought that news of her arrival would be all over town within the hour. She accepted the key from the clerk's extended hand and taking her valise, walked up the stairs to the second floor. Her room was toward the far end of the hallway.

The room was small, but accommodating. A stale odor hung lightly in the air. Long faded blue curtains outlined the single window overlooking Main Street. There was a single bed, a nightstand with oil lamp, and a chair stood next to the window. A small dresser with mirror stood against the opposite wall with a basin and pitcher of water. A washcloth and hand towel lay next to it. A large bath towel lay folded on the foot of the bed.

Laura placed her valise on the chair and removed her jacket and hat, hanging them on the back of the chair. She opened the window to air out the stale odor before examining herself in the mirror. She reflected on the haggard-looking young woman that gazed back at her. She was tired and it showed in her eyes. Laura stood mesmerized until a light rap at the door snapped her back to the present.

"Who is it?" she asked somewhat dryly.

"It's Johnny from the stage depot with your trunk," was the muffled reply.

Laura moved to the door, opened it and smiled slightly. There stood a blonde-headed boy of about seventeen years dressed in overalls and faded blue shirt. He had Laura's trunk in tow.

"Hi, Miss Sumner, I'm Johnny Sedwick. I work at the stage depot after school. The boss said to bring this here trunk to your room."

"Just set it down at the foot of the bed, Johnny, "she instructed, while searching her purse for a few coins to show her appreciation. Johnny complied with her wishes and turned to go. She stopped him with a quick few words, "Wait, Johnny. Here—for your trouble. Thank you very much."

Johnny blushed, but took the coins and quickly glancing at them in his hand, smiled, and sheepishly backed out of the door. He closed it softly behind him. Laura smiled in amusement. The small token she had given him had made his day.

Laura locked the door and moved to the window. She peered down into the street to watch for several minutes as people went about their evening business. Thoughts of Uncle Jesse entered her mind as she glanced up and down the street. Fond remembrances of accompanying him to the general store, the bank, and the livery stable came to her mind. Laura suddenly felt very tired so decided that she would take a short nap before going to a café for supper. She sat on the bed and removed her shoes to massage her feet. She lay down on the bed and within moments was asleep, visions of her uncle floating through her mind.

An hour and a half passed before Laura opened her crystal blue eyes to fading shadows on the walls. She stretched fully, then, lay still for a long moment before rising to put her shoes back on. From somewhere down the street she could hear the melody of a piano in a saloon as the player plinked out the lively strains of *De Camp Town Ladies*. Laura smiled as she hummed the tune softly while she finished dressing for supper.

A little over an hour later, Laura returned to the hotel room and lit the oil lamp on the nightstand. She pulled the window shade down, drew the curtains half closed and prepared for bed. As she turned out the lamp and lay back on the bed, thoughts of the morrow crept into her mind. The young woman from Texas drifted off into a restless sleep.

*   *   *

The next morning, Laura was up with the crowing of a distant rooster and the aroma of bacon frying in the cafés. After a quick breakfast with coffee, she walked down to Lawyer Yates' office. The sign on the door indicated that he had not yet arrived to work. Laura sat down on a bench outside the law office. She crossed her arms and tapped her foot a bit, anxious to get started. Within minutes, a middle-aged man in a suit stepped out of the boarding house across the street and walked toward her. Laura took a deep breath and exhaled. Yes, this was Lawyer Yates. The man reached for the key in his pocket as he stepped to the door and smiled at Laura.

"Good morning to you." he said as he opened the door, "Do you have business with me?" Laura smiled back at him and replied, "Yes, if you are Wilbur Yates, then I indeed have business with you."

Allowing Laura to step through the door ahead of him, Yates motioned Laura to a chair in front of his desk while he hung up his jacket and donned a pair of spectacles. He then inquired as to who she was and what business she had with him. Laura produced the letter she received from him saying, "You sent this to me. I am Laura Sumner."

Yates nodded slightly, "Yes, of course, Miss Sumner, I heard last night that you had arrived. First of all, please accept my deepest sympathy for the loss of your Uncle Jesse Sumner. He was a fine man and well liked in these parts." Laura immediately thought, "That's the second person that's said that about Uncle Jesse. If he was so well liked, then why was he killed?"

Yates rose and moved to a file cabinet where he quickly found the appropriate folder, then returned to his desk. He studied the documents for a few minutes, clearing his voice before speaking, "Miss Sumner, your uncle came to me about three months ago and retained me to write his last will and testament. In this document he left all of his holdings to you. You are now the legal owner of the Sumner horse ranch. The bank holds a note on the property for one thousand dollars. There are a few other debts that must be settled as well. Once you take possession of the property, you will have ninety days to pay all of these debts in full. Now, please sign this document for me, assuring that you are Laura Sumner and that you are taking possession of the said property." Yates presented Laura with the legal document.

Laura read the paper carefully and then, taking quill pen in hand, signed it and handed it back to him. Yates then asked if she was going directly to the ranch. She replied, "I'd like to speak with the sheriff first to see what has been done about finding those responsible for murdering my uncle. Then I will rent a buggy to go to the ranch."

"Of course, Miss Sumner, I'll walk with you to the sheriff's office and then to the livery to rent your wagon." Yates thought for a moment before saying, "Perhaps I should get someone to drive you out to the ranch. This is still a wild country here-a-bouts."

Laura grinned a bit and answered, "Mr. Yates, I grew up on a farm and can handle a team. I can also shoot. I think that I can take care of myself." Yates looked surprised but kept his tongue.

Sheriff Jack Wakely looked up from his desk as Laura and Wilbur Yates entered the jail. He was of medium height and strongly built, with a stern face. "What can I do for you?" he asked gruffly, although Laura's arrival in town was already common knowledge.

Lawyer Yates answered, "Miss Sumner here is the benefactor of ole Jesse Sumner's ranch. She came to inquire about your investigation into Jesse's death."

Jack Wakely leaned back in his chair, and looking Laura up and down appraisingly, replied, "We went out to the place where they found him. There were some tracks, but they suddenly disappeared over hard rocky ground. We searched wide circles but never found those tracks again. Whoever done it is long gone out of this territory. We never found hide nor hair of Jesse's horses either. I'm afraid there's not much more we can do."

Laura watched the sheriff's eyes as he spoke and she didn't like what she saw. Jack Wakely was lying, and she knew it. Laura felt that the sheriff knew more than he was telling and that there was something foreboding in his voice. She didn't trust him, nor did she trust his deputies, especially Forgy—the deputy that Uncle Jesse pointed out during her previous visit. Laura knew that she had do something. She wanted justice in this matter and it wasn't going to come from the likes of Jack Wakely.

Later this evening she would write to the United States Marshal and request an investigation. For the moment though, Laura only nodded her head. She forced a smile, saying "Thank you, Sheriff, I'll be taking over Uncle Jesse's ranch and building up that horse herd again." She watched Wakely's eyes at her announcement, and he didn't appear pleased about it. Rising from her chair, Laura turned to Wilbur. "Come, Mr. Yates, let's get to the livery and that buggy."

At the livery stable, Laura rented a one-horse buggy then drove it to the hotel where she got the porter to load her trunk in the boot of the wagon. Thoughtfully, Laura glanced toward the general store as food came to mind. "I may just need a few days' staples at the ranch," she decided. She climbed into the buggy, clucked to the bay horse, turned the buggy around in the center of the street and drove to the entrance of the store.

Once inside, she found that grocery items were stocked along the right side and dry goods stocked along the left. Hardware items were stored along the back wall. A barrel of crackers stood near a potbellied stove in the center of the store, and a few men sat in wooden chairs enjoying male habits and conversing in generalities. Various other kegs and barrels were lined in rows through the center of the store and contained fresh or salted items including cheeses, jerked meats, and pickled fish.

Laura took up a straw basket and selected a tin of Arbuckle's coffee, a few large potatoes, a small sack of snap beans, a few ears of corn, a loaf of freshly baked bread, slices of ham, beef, a pound of flour, and a pound of sugar. Then, she stepped to the counter where a tall, lanky, apron-clad clerk awaited her. Laura placed the basket on the counter and the clerk tallied up her purchase.

"I should like to open a line of credit with your store," announced Laura when the clerk voiced the total.

"Certainly, Miss, do you have a means of support in this town?" inquired the clerk.

Laura looked him straight in the eyes and related, "I am Laura Sumner. I've just acquired the Sumner ranch and will be working it."

Momentarily, the din of banter from around the store fell hushed. The clerk swallowed hard. Before he could respond, behind Laura came a male voice, "Miss Sumner, I am John Talbot, proprietor. The Sumner outfit still owes me for two month's supplies and I have cut off their credit. Seeing as you are newly arrived, I will grant you a line of credit equal to what you purchase today. You will have to bring the Sumner account up-to-date within the week in order to extend further credit."

Laura flushed slightly but answered him directly to his face, "Mr. Talbot, in that case, I will pay for my purchases today in cash and will secure your arrears with haste."

That startled Talbot and he was speechless. A few customers grinned at her fortitude. Laura then turned to the clerk and with a second thought, also purchased a double-barreled shotgun along with two boxes of shells.

The clerk helped her load the items into the buggy. Once settled, Laura loaded the shotgun and positioned it at her side. Then, she chuckled to the bay and turned the wagon toward the west end of town to drive the hour to her ranch—her destiny.

CHAPTER NINE

The Sumner Ranch

It was near to an hour of riding when Laura Lynn Sumner stopped the rented buggy at the entrance to Sumner Ranch. Upon leaving the main stagecoach road, the narrow trail passed under a simple wooden archway constructed of two upright poles that held a crossbar. From the crossbar was suspended a sign with Sumner Ranch crudely burned into it.

Laura sat motionless at the gate to survey the surrounding area. The foothills of the Rocky Mountains were just to the left of her and ahead lay Jesse Sumner's land in a small valley with a sparkling stream near the house, stable, bunkhouse, and corrals.

The buildings sat less than a hundred yards ahead of her. All was quiet on the ranch; however, she could see a few men sitting around outside the bunkhouse. Although she observed a few horses in the corrals, there appeared to be no work being done and that bothered her.

Laura took a deep breath, exhaled, and then slapped the reins to the bay, and the horse broke into a brisk trot. Laura's heart thumped all the way to the hitching rack in front of the house where she halted, climbed out of the buggy, looped the reins around the post, then tied it securely.

Turning around toward the bunkhouse, she found five men walking toward her. She recognized four of them as working for Jesse when she last visited. "Laura!" exclaimed Tom Baker, the oldest of the group. "We didn't think that you would come back." The others huddled around. There was Chad Granger, Josh Barton, Sam Gratton, and the youngest wrangler, a disheveled-looking man new to Laura. He was introduced as Lyle Turner. Turner had only been with the ranch days before Jesse was killed.

"Tom, what is going on here?" Laura asked. "There should be a lot of horses being worked. This spread needs money to pay the bills."

"Well, Laura," began Tom, frowning "we found horses three different times since Jesse was killed, and we brought them back here to work. They were rustled in the middle of the night, and although we followed the trail, it disappeared in the same area where Jesse's body was found. We just don't know what to do. The sheriff was here with a message for us to stay put because the bank would soon own this land, and then, the banker would pay us our back wages. So, here we are just a waiting for something to happen."

"Something did happen, Tom," replied Laura. "Uncle Jesse willed all his holdings to me. I am the legal owner of this ranch now and I intend to turn it into a good place to live and work. I want to build a herd to raise horses and train them to saddle. I want the best horse ranch in the territory, and we are going to start first thing in the morning. Are you all ready?" Laura searched each of their faces and was unsettled at what she saw.

Lyle Turner was the first to speak up. "The hell you say! I ain't riding for no woman. It takes a man to run a ranch, and if a man don't run this spread, I won't stay."

Laura looked at Turner and announced, "Turner, collect your gear and get out. I won't have shirkers working for me." Turner stared hard at Laura and started to rebut, but thought better of it. He turned on his heels and headed for the bunkhouse to get his gear. Laura turned to Tom saying, "Tom, please make sure he is off this land by sundown. I am going to get situated in the house, then go over all of Jesse's papers. After I've gotten my things into the house, please unhitch the buggy and take care of the horse. We will talk more in the morning."

Tom nodded his understanding, then turned to Josh and told him to take care of the buggy and stable the animal. Both Tom and Sam Gratton took up Laura's trunk and supplies and followed her into the house. Chad Granger strode over to the bunkhouse to keep watch on Turner.

Tom spoke again to Laura, "The house has not been touched since Jesse's burial. We laid him to rest up on that low knoll in back of the house." There was a musty odor to the house so Laura had the boys open all the windows to air it out.

She went to the room that she occupied during her previous visit and, to her amazement, found it exactly as she had left it. Her horse hunting and working outfit had been laundered and was laid out across the foot of the bed. Uncle Jesse, it seemed, knew that she would be coming back. Tears filled Laura's eyes.

After the boys left her to her own devices, Laura went to the hill to visit Uncle Jesse's grave. The boys had made a crude headboard with his name and birth year along with the inscription, "Murdered May 10, 1873." Laura was sad that the grave was barren. She would place some wildflowers on it tomorrow.

Laura returned to the house and moved slowly from room to room as memories of her beloved Uncle Jesse sifted through her mind. Sometimes she smiled, and sometimes she wiped a tear with her handkerchief. Finally, she dried her eyes and went to her room. A sense of warmth enveloped her and she took off her jacket and hat, laying them on a chair. She realized that she was hungry and went to the kitchen area to make a sandwich of beef and bread.

After the meager meal, Laura went to Jesse's desk and gathered up all of his financial documents. She lit the coal oil lamp and studied them for a long time. Ledgers showed that Jesse had a plan and that plan included a large herd of horses to sell to the Army. If that had happened, then all the bills would have been paid. The rustling activities sorely interfered with Jesse's plan.

Laura sat quietly with her thoughts for a long time, then she took paper and quill pen in hand and with steadfast resolve, wrote a letter to the U.S. Marshal in Denver.

To The United States Marshal, Colorado Territory

June 20, 1873

I have recently inherited my Uncle Jesse Sumner's ranch due to his murder at the hands of unknown rustlers. I have inquired of the local law, Sheriff Jack Wakely, the circumstances of my uncle's death and am not satisfied with his explanation. I suspect that the sheriff has falsified information and that unless your intervention is eminent, justice will not be served. Therefore, I request that your office conduct an investigation into my uncle's death as well as the ongoing rustling activity.

I remain,

Yours respectively,

Laura Sumner
Sumner Ranch
Lower Colorado Territory

Laura then sealed the letter in an envelope and addressed it. She would ensure its delivery in the morning. Now she was tired. She went to her room and undressed to her chemise. After washing up a bit, she slipped into bed and within minutes was sound asleep. Visions of a vast herd of multi-colored mustangs roamed through her mind and a slight smile formed around her mouth.

*   *   *

Laura rose early with the sun just peeking over the hills to the east. She washed up in the washroom basin and dressed in her horse hunting outfit of men's Levi's, blue linen shirt open at the collar, boots, spurs, and rumpled black Stetson. She donned her chaps and tied a light blue bandana loosely around her neck. At her waist, she buckled the hand-tooled gunbelt that Jesse made for her and after checking the loads, slipped her Colt Lighting revolver into the holster. She was ready for the tasks at hand and the first thing was to make sure that her letter would get to Denver. She was afraid that if she mailed the letter in town, Jack Wakely would get his hands on it. No, that wouldn't happen. She would ride out to the stagecoach road and personally hand the letter to the driver and ask him to deliver it. Once done, she would address the wranglers, and appraise them of what she envisioned as the future of the ranch.

Laura went to the stable and looked over the horses. She found Brandy, the amber-colored mare that Jesse let her ride during her last visit in the third stall. She also found her saddle, bridle and trappings. Laura saddled up Brandy and led her out of the stable where she mounted and rode out the gate toward the stagecoach road that led north to the territorial capital. After an hour's wait, the northbound coach rumbled toward her.

Laura hailed the coach to stop as it drew closer. She recognized the driver of the coach from her last trip and greeted him with a smile as she handed him up the addressed envelope, asking, "Good morning, Mr. Tandy. What might the postage be to deliver this letter to Denver?"

The driver looked over the address and replied, "Well, Miss Sumner, this letter weighs just about one full ounce, so at the rate of three cents per half ounce, the mailing cost should be a total of six cents." Laura reached into her jeans pocket and produced two 1870 U.S. Silver 3 cent pieces and handed them up to Tandy who nodded approval as he tucked the money and the letter into his inside vest pocket.

John Tandy then waved farewell as he once again took up the reins and his whip. There was a sharp snap as he loudly voiced his command to the team, "Getup there! Come on hosses, we got to get to Denver on time! Hee-Haw!" The team surged into the harnesses and the coach lumbered away. Laura watched it disappear for a few minutes, then turned Brandy back toward the Sumner ranch.

The four remaining wranglers were just saddling up when Laura returned. They each gave her an apprising look, nodding their approval of her working outfit. When they were all mounted, Laura turned to Tom asking, "Where is the best area to hunt wild horses today?"

Tom replied, "Jesse always said that the place to go and track was to the west of here, in the foothills to the Rockies."

Laura nodded, "Then, that's where we will go," and she led out toward the blue shadowed distance.

Hours ticked by and by noon they still hadn't found any tracks nor sighted any wild horses so the small party rested beside a creek while their mounts watered and grazed. "I think that we should split up, we can cover more ground that way," announced Tom. Laura looked over each of their faces and the others were nodding their agreement.

"All right," said Laura, "we'll split into three groups. Tom, you and Chad go north. Josh and Sam go south, and I will continue west for the next few hours, then turn north to meet with Tom and Chad. After two hours southward, Josh and Sam will turn back toward the ranch. We should all meet there by dusk."

Laura mounted Brandy and watched the others turn to their assigned directions. She took a deep breath with a silent prayer during her exhale, then lightly touched Brandy with her spurs and crossed the creek heading west.

At the two hour mark, Laura was amongst the roughest country she had ever seen. There were large boulders, trees, heavy brush, and steep slopes. Twice, she had to dismount and lead Brandy up a slope, then rest for long minutes before remounting and continuing her hunt.

Finally, she bottomed out from a long slope and found herself along a stream that she assumed was a tributary of the Arkansas River. She rode slowly to the banks of the babbling creek where she found tracks in the muddy shoreline. There were a lot of tracks and they were unshod. "Horses!" thought Laura. "And not too long ago." She followed them into the creek and up the embankment on the other side. The tracks turned north and she did likewise.

Within the hour, Laura topped a steep rise and in the distance she could just barely make out a large multi-colored blob moving fast along a ridge. She touched spur to Brandy and rode quickly to close the distance. Minutes ticked away before Laura finally observed two other riders driving hard to catch the evasive animals.

Suddenly, Laura watched in horror as the lead rider's horse stumbled and went down nose first, rolling over the hapless rider. She swallowed hard as she urged Brandy forward to the scene. The wild herd escaped as the second rider pulled up and dismounted to render aid to the fallen man.

Minutes later, Laura was beside them, dismounting in a flurry and looking down ashen-faced at the crushed body of Tom Baker. Tom was dead and his horse was floundering to get up with a broken leg and broken back. There was nothing anyone could do.

Laura looked into Chad Granger's disbelieving eyes and said, "Chad, shoot the horse and we'll rig a travois to take Tom and his trappings back to the ranch." It was a long, silent trail back.

Laura and Tad reached the ranch at dusk. Josh and Sam were already back, feeling satisfied with twenty head of horses including a roan stallion, some mares, a few colts, fillies, and foals. They had placed the captured horses in the large corral. Both men turned somber when they learned about Tom's demise. They carried his blanket-wrapped remains to the tool shed for burial the next day, close to Jesse.

The next day at just after noon, Tom was laid to rest on the knoll near Jesse. He had on his best outfit and was wrapped in a favorite blanket. Laura read the Bible and they sang *Rock of Ages* before sealing the grave and placing a crude marker with his name and statistics on it. Because of the sadness, Laura elected not to hunt horses this day, but to return to that task the next morning. She picked wildflowers to lay at each grave before returning to the house where she lay down for a while, attempting to gather her thoughts.

Later that evening, Laura once again went over Jesse's papers to see if she might have missed something in her first assessment. In her mind, Laura outlined her own plan to put the ranch on its feet and to keep improving the property. She surmised that at some point, the abundance of wild stock would dwindle to almost nothing. She knew that she had to start breeding the best of the stock to build a good ranch. The ranch needed the best of the catches to retain as sires and breeders, and to that end, she was adamant. Like her uncle, Laura knew that she must put her plan on paper soon. It would be the foundation of her future.

Unbeknown to Laura, a serious discussion was underway in the bunkhouse. The three remaining wranglers were leery of the latest happenings at the ranch—missing stock, Jesse Sumner's murder, the sheriff's warnings, Laura's arrival, and now; Tom Baker's accidental demise. It shaped up to be a bad omen for them and each voiced his opinion. In the end, they determined that they would all leave in the night and each take one additional saddle horse for compensation. Laura would have to work it out by herself and maybe she would give up and go back to Texas. The men would find work on other ranches in the area.

Laura rose early the next morning and after dressing in her working outfit as before, she went to the stables only to find that all three of the remaining wranglers' horses were gone. Puzzled, she went to the bunkhouse and found it empty. The wranglers had deserted her during the night. She was now alone to work the ranch singlehandedly. The men, at least, had left the twenty horses that must be broken to saddle. However, each had taken a second tamed horse from the stable. That was money to anyone, and she correctly surmised that it was to make up for overdue wages.

Laura sat down on the bench in front of the bunkhouse and tried to think clearly. What could she do? What could one lone woman do to continue? She closed her eyes and hung her head in silence for long minutes. It came to her. She knew what she had to do. She would not be run off, rather would work her plan to save the ranch and her destiny.

Laura got up from the bench and set her mind to the task at hand. She needed to be stubborn to the bone. She walked to the corral and taking up a lariat, picked out the first horse, a bay colt, to work. She roped it and moved it to the work corral. Work would focus her mind on something besides bad omens.

Laura slipped a hackamore bridle over the colt's head and tied the bay to a post of the corral. She then loosened her bandana and slipping it off, tied it around the colt's eyes. She got a saddle and saddle blanket and while speaking softly to the animal, placed them onto the horse's back. It shivered a bit but Laura was patient. She let the animal get used to the weight for several minutes. Still talking in soft tones, she cinched up. The horse fidgeted and sidestepped as she completed the task. Sweat stung her eyes, burned her face and trickled down her body as she worked. She left the horse standing alone while she went to the water trough and splashed water on her face, letting it drip down her neck into her shirt. It felt cool as she inhaled deeply and exhaled with a long rush.

Laura stood at the corral bars with a cup of water, watching the animal's movements as it stood blindfolded, pondering the unfamiliar weight on its back. Finally, she set down the cup and climbed over the corral bars, walking warily toward the bay while speaking softly. "It's time," she thought. "It's now or never."

Laura moved to the left side of the colt and taking the hackamore reins in her hand, put foot to stirrup and swung quickly into the saddle. She felt the horse tense and knew it was going to be all or none. She grasped the bandana with her right hand and quickly removed it from the horse's eyes.

A split second later Laura was riding high as the colt suddenly bucked hind quarters high in the air coming down with a bone-jarring jolt. She gritted her teeth as the next jolt came before the colt went into a twisting motion. The bay hopped in circles trying to throw the strange weight that struggled to stay put.

Long minutes ticked away as the lithe woman unrelentingly jerked, bounced, swayed, and jarred with the wild bucking whirlwind of muscle and bone to finally become one with each other. Finally, the bay stood still, seemingly waiting for instructions.

Laura lightly touched his flank with a spur and worked the reins as the newly broken colt moved to her wishes. She rode him to the gate and dismounted. For several minutes, she spoke to the horse in a calm voice. At last, Laura just dropped the reins and walked around the corral. The colt followed closely behind her.

Stabling the bay, Laura saw the buggy that she rented from the livery. She needed to return it and today would be best. She got the rental horse from its stall and hitched up the buggy. She saddled up Brandy and tied her to the rear of the wagon, so she could ride Brandy back to the ranch.

Stopping momentarily at the house for some money and her shotgun, she also got Uncle Jesse's Henry repeating rifle from over the fireplace and slid it into her saddle scabbard. It was good to be prepared. As she drove the wagon through the gate toward the stagecoach road, a sudden chill ran down Laura's spine and she slowly studied the landscape around her. She could see nothing out of the ordinary, but the hair on the back of her neck seemed to stiffen. It was as though she was being watched from a distance. She knew that she would have to be infinitely careful.

*   *   *

Numerous people watched Laura as she drove the buggy down Main Street of Miller's Station to the livery stable. After taking care of that business, she took Brandy by the reins and walked to the general store. She could hear muffled voices talking as they took in her less than feminine attire. It was considered improper for a woman to wear men's garb. At one point in her walk, she thought that she recognized Josh Barton, one of her deserter wranglers sitting on a bench outside a saloon. She looked straight at the man, but he hung his head in avoidance and she couldn't definitely say that it was he.

At the general store, Laura tied Brandy to the hitching post and entered, her spurs jingling with each step. She took her time shopping for the essentials that she needed before stepping to the counter. After paying the clerk, she turned to the whispering men around the potbellied stove and spoke in a clear voice, "Certain men may have deserted me, but I am no quitter. I am staying put. I am going to work the Sumner ranch and make it pay."

She hesitated with the ensuing silence, letting her words sink in for a moment. Then she continued, "If there is any good man who knows horses and will work for a woman with the promise of being paid, then send him out to me. I need good men."

With that announcement, Laura turned on her heels and left the store. A busy buzz of discussion ensued upon her departure. In the dimness of the store, a lone woman smiled her admiration for Laura.

Among those who watched Laura depart town was the sheriff. Jack Wakley scowled as she rode past his office and he thought, "She looks like she's going to try and stay here. Just what will it take to send her packing?"

Laura arrived back at the ranch without incident. She felt that there was still time to start working the next horse and so she picked another colt, a sorrel with blazed face. She repeated her initial actions with this second animal, but this one was tougher and twice she was thrown and had to painfully climb back into the saddle to continue. By day's end, she still had not broken this fiery beast. Needing to rest and contend with various bruises and aching body, she stabled the colt, vowing to tame him the very next day.

A hot bath was in order and so Laura spent the next hour dumping buckets of heated water into the galvanized tub in the washroom. The soaking felt good and the liniment afterward took the edge off. After a sparse supper of beans, bacon, biscuits, and coffee, Laura checked to make sure all windows were down and locked, and bolted the doors. She carried the oil lamp into her bedroom and dressed for bed. The last thing she did before retiring and slipping into slumber was to lay her Colt Lightning on the stand next to her bed—within reach.

During the ensuing days, Laura doggedly worked horse after horse until they were broken to saddle. One by one, she turned them to pasture within close proximity of the house. Her small herd was growing, but she needed a lot more horses and the day finally came that she had to mount up alone to hunt down more wild stock.

Thus it began, Laura now dressed in her horse hunting outfit every day. Levi's, denim shirt, black Stetson, boots, spurs, and chaps were her uniform. The gunbelt, slung close to hand as Uncle Jesse had taught her was always with her. Laura Lynne Sumner had transitioned into the *horsewoman* of her Uncle's description.

CHAPTER TEN

Enter The Law

Judge Joshua Bernard Wilkerson frowned as he reread the letter before him. The letter was addressed to the United States Marshal, and sent by a woman named Laura Sumner. The most disturbing thing to him about the letter was that local law enforcement officials seemed to have done nothing credible to solve the rustling problem nor had they solved the murder of a prominent citizen. Those facts troubled him.

He rose from his desk and, moving to a long table across the room, rummaged through a stack of old newspapers until he found the one that he wanted. Returning to his desk, he thumbed through the paper until he found the article that he recalled reading, the one about the murder of Jesse Sumner.

The judge reread the article, pondered the few details provided, then went to the door of his office and called out, "Henry! Check your files and bring me all the information that you have on capital crime cases in the Lower Colorado area. More specifically, I want all the cases from the town of Miller's Station."

It took only fifteen minutes before Henry appeared before the judge with a single sheet of paper in his hand. "Judge Wilkerson, you aren't going to believe this, but the one and only case from that area was tried over five years ago, before your time here. There have not been any prisoners brought in from that area since that time."

Wilkerson formed his hands together in steeple fashion, placed them over his lips and silently looked over his rimmed spectacles at Henry for a very long minute. "Henry, get me all the information that you can find on a sheriff there named Jack Wakely. I want to know everything there is on that man."

"Yessir!" came the reply as Henry dutifully scurried back into the court administrative office. Judge Wilkerson's mind worked like a finely tuned machine and right now, he did not like what he was thinking.

Within the hour, Henry reappeared in the judge's office. "Judge, it seems that this man Jack Wakely became sheriff by appointment of the town council right after the previous sheriff, George Simms, was crippled in a freak wagon accident. There is an indication that he hails from Missouri and that he rode with Quantrill's guerillas." Judge Wilkerson nodded his understanding before quickly asking, "Who is the next Deputy Marshal up for assignment?"

"Cole Stockton is available, Sir," replied Henry.

"Get him for me straight away, Henry. Go right now to get Cole Stockton and bring him to my office."

"Yessir! Right away!" Henry turned on his heels and was out the door. Judge Wilkerson pondered the evidence, "Wakely rode with Quantrill—raiders. I'd bet that he's now leading a band of thieves, cutthroats, and murderers, but we shall see."

*   *   *

I had risen with the first crowing of a rooster somewhere in the neighborhood of my boarding house and had a bite to eat and coffee in the dining room before seeing to my roan, Chino. Just now, I was sitting back in a wooden chair in the jail, enjoying a good cup of coffee and jawing with Sheriff Donovan and a deputy. Our lively discussion was suddenly interrupted by the appearance of Henry, Judge Wilkerson's clerk.

"Marshal Stockton, I am glad to find you so quick. The judge wants to see you straightaway. He has a situation that demands immediate attention, and I was sent to bring you with haste."

Well, I'd learned one thing in the past six or seven weeks of being a Deputy U.S. Marshal for Judge Wilkerson, and that was when he called for you, he expected a prompt response. I rose from the wooden armchair, finished the bit of coffee in my cup and set it on a table. "Alright, Henry, let's go see the judge." Fifteen minutes later, Henry admitted me to the judge's office. He was anxious to see me.

"Marshal Stockton, thank you for coming so quickly. I have a situation here that demands our utmost attention. Let me read a letter to you that was recently passed to me." Judge Wilkerson read the letter aloud. When he finished, he took a few moments to reflect, then offered his surmise, "Cole, there is something rotten down along the passes at Miller's Station and we are going to sort out the apple barrel and rid the town of the bad ones."

Reflecting myself, on past events, I recalled that I had met Mr. Sumner in the wilds and shared a camp with him when I was hunting down the killer Charlie Sturgis. I said as much to Judge Wilkerson. His reply was such that it was good that I was somewhat familiar with that territory, because as he put it, "I want you to leave first thing in the morning and travel incognito; that means hide your badge until you have the facts straight. When you deem it appropriate, you will identify yourself and arrest all that are involved with this travesty. I want those responsible for the murder of Jesse Sumner and the horse rustling to answer for their transgressions. You are the instrument of justice."

That word *justice* cut to the heart. I knew what the judge was thinking. There was going to be gunplay involved with it. I nodded my understanding. We rose from our chairs and the judge showed me to the door. "Good hunting, Marshal Stockton," he bid me as I left his chamber.

I left the courthouse and went directly to Robertson's Mercantile & Emporium, since I needed a few supplies to make this trip. Ammunition was foremost on my list, not to mention some Arbuckle coffee and beef jerky. I knew that I could use a couple pairs of new socks also. It seems that my big toes were starting to sneak through the end of my present pair. Anyway, I'd browse the store and get a few things for my tote sack.

*   *   *

It was still dark when I rose and donned my traveling clothes, namely dark blue shirt with faded yellow bandana, Levi's, rumpled dark coat, worn but comfortable boots, and spurs. I slipped my marshal's star into the inside pocket of my jacket. Following a quick breakfast, the early morning found me riding south on Chino, my big roan, toward the passes of southern Colorado.

Riding alone in nature gives a man time to think. I had more than enough time to do that since it would take me a few days travel to Miller's Station. I figured that I would have a plan of action by the time that I got there. Somehow, I kept going over and over in my mind the conversation that ole Jesse Sumner and I had some months ago. I also thought about that letter that Laura Sumner wrote, as well as the judge's interpretation. It would be best if I stayed shy of the local law while I surveyed the situation. I hoped that no one would recognize me before I had made a thorough investigation.

I had not shaved in a week by the time I arrived in Miller's Station. I could certainly pass for a down-on-my-luck drifter, which was the way that I wanted it. I had already decided to spend a day or so in town just lazing and watching. I learned long ago that the best places to listen and observe are the livery, barbershop, saloons, and the general store.

After I got Chino situated at the livery, I inquired of the hostler as to where I might lay my head for a night or so for very low rates. He advised that he had a small back room with a bunk that I could rent for fifty cents a night. That fit the bill in my present guise so I forked over one night's lodging in advance. Deciding that a cool beer would cut the dust from my throat, I strolled down the main street to the nearest purveyor of fine spirits.

I stopped momentarily at the entrance to the Honey Bee Saloon to beat some dust off my jeans with my Stetson, then shuffled up to the bar. The barkeep was prompt in taking my order and while he drew a mug of cool beer from that keg, I helped myself to one of the free meat and cheese sandwiches stacked on a plate at the end of the bar.

Taking my beer and sandwich, I moved to an inconspicuous table toward the rear of the room. In this location, I was able to observe all of the activity. There were a few miners and some townsmen, as well as a couple of guys who looked to be cowhands or wranglers.

These gents were speaking in low voices, but I overheard enough to place them as out-of-work horse wranglers. It seems that they had last worked on the Sumner ranch. From their talk, I was able to get the gist of Miss Sumner's situation, and it didn't sound good. They also let it out that they were expecting to get paid when she quit the ranch. They were pretty sure that it would be very soon. I filed that information away in the back of my mind.

I finished the beer and sandwich before deciding to drop in at the general store. Just as I started out the bat-wing doors of the saloon, a stocky deputy sheriff pushed inward. We sort've locked doors on each other. Our eyes held for a moment. He stared at me with venom in his eyes. "Look out where you're going, Mister," he snapped.

Not wishing to be out of line with the law, I replied, "Pardon me, Deputy," and stepped out of his way. He brushed roughly past me and walked to the bar. By habit, I took note of his hardware and how he wore it. There were four notches carved on the grip of his pistol and he swaggered as he walked. I figured him for what he was—a tinhorn dandy putting on a show.

Leaving the saloon, I crossed the street and stepped up on the boardwalk to the general store. A quick glance through the window confirmed several customers shopping as well as the proverbial *cracker barrel bunch.* I stepped inside and browsed the shelves as though seeking something in particular. I found this store well stocked. There were some cheeses and crackers for sampling so I helped myself to a few.

The ole boys sitting around the potbellied stove were talking about the news of the day. There was talk of the rustling activity: mainly about trails followed by the sheriff and his posse, apparently in search of rustlers, but that the tracks were lost in rocky, mountainous terrain. Like those before in the saloon, they also exchanged thoughts and opinions about that young woman, Laura Sumner, speculating as to whether or not she would stay on that ranch or sell out and be gone.

One statement in particular caught my attention. It seems that Laura Sumner was looking to hire good wranglers but no one in this town would help. Well, I'd broken a few horses to saddle in my time and to be right on that ranch when things happened just suited me to a tee. I would ride out there and try to get hired after surveying the town situation.

After the general store, I moved over to the stagecoach and express station. A body could sit there on a bench for some time without raising too much suspicion and it was close to the sheriff's office. I wanted to see just how this law operated. Periodically deputies would come and go at the jail and I counted at least five who wore stars on their shirts and vests.

Finally, around supper time, the sheriff himself left the jail and walked over to the café. I decided to follow suit to learn some firsthand information on this man. As usual, I took in the manner of how he wore his gun. He wore his rig low to the wrist and tied down for a faster draw. He walked confidently and people seemed to avert their eyes from his. Plus, they moved out of his way without speaking as he approached. This man was a bully.

Once inside the café, I took a window table so I could observe the street as well as the man with the sheriff's star on his chest. He sat by himself but carefully watched the clientele as he sipped coffee and waited for his supper. I ordered up a couple of thick pork chops with potatoes, gravy, beans, and bread. The coffee was good.

After the meal, I stepped out to the street. Dusk was upon us now and several horses lined the hitching racks at all of the watering holes. Ranch hands were in town for liquid refreshment, a hand or two of cards, or perhaps a dance with one of the saloon girls. Lively piano music drifted from the saloons. I soon recognized the strains of *Buffalo Gals* as I once again took the bench outside the stage depot. I took up a stick lying next to the bench and got out my pocketknife to try my hand at whittling a bit while I watched the evening activities.

Later that evening, the street became quite lively. This is the time when most arguments commence and most drunks stagger out into the night air. That's when I observed the sheriff and five deputies emerge from the jail and move to the saloons. It occurred to me that six lawmen were too many for the size of this town.

It wasn't long before two deputies hauled a guy out of the batwings and around the corner into the alley. There was a muffled struggle before the two lawmen dragged the limp form, pockets turned wrong-side out, to the jailhouse. I surmised what happened. They had beaten him unconscious, then, rifled through his pockets before arresting him. The same thing happened about a half hour later.

I now understood how the sheriff made his money. Well, I'd seen enough to know that the law here-a-bouts was not on the up and up. I would do something about that before I left the community. A good night's sleep was in order now so I moved to the livery and that bunk. Sometime tomorrow, I would ride out to the Sumner ranch and meet this Laura Sumner.

*   *   *

It wasn't the best of bunks that I slept in that night: it being just a mite better than the hard ground, but I made do. I slept fairly well considering horses moving around stalls and town sounds until early morning. Nonetheless, I was an early riser and as the sun threw the first rays upon the peaks of the Rocky Mountains to the west of town, I was up and stripped to the waist at a washbasin out back of the livery. I dearly wanted to shave this morning, but my present masquerade would not allow it yet. There would be time for that later. Right now, all I wanted was to clean up and change my soggy socks. My shirt could use changing also.

I rummaged through my tote bag and came up with a pair of dry socks, ones that I had bought before leaving Denver. I also found a somewhat wrinkled and faded red shirt. When you are traveling, it doesn't make much difference how you start out the day; those wrinkles will work themselves out.

I saw to Chino, filling a wooden bucket with water, pitching some hay into his feed box and lacing it with a scoop of grain. He liked it and muzzled his appreciation before putting on the feed bag. That reminded me that I needed some nourishment also. So, after strapping on my hardware and settling it in place, I walked down to the first café where I'd had supper last night.

The saloons were not yet opened, but the town was awake with business owners sweeping off the boardwalk in front of their establishments. Customers wandered around in the various shops. I took special note of the jail as deputies were turning out the drunks from the previous night. Those that argued about missing money were told to chalk it up to being drunk and spending it all. Well, there was nothing I could do for those poor cheated cowboys right now, and I could smell the bacon frying and biscuits baking. My stomach seemed to growl out a hunger for something nourishing.

When I entered the café, I observed that same stocky deputy sitting at a far table and ogling the pretty waitress as she filled orders. She paid him no mind; however, I could see that he was getting on her nerves. She was relieved when another deputy entered behind me and advised, "Hey Forgy! Sheriff Wakley wants to see you right now." Forgy gulped down his coffee and hurriedly left the establishment. Once again, I took a seat near the window. Momentarily the young waitress was beside me. I ordered up and she smiled at me before she turned to place my order.

After breakfast I wandered down to the general store. A rancher was there talking to others about some missing stock. While I stood around the hardware counter looking over the latest models of Colt and Remington revolvers, Sheriff Wakley entered the store and was immediately hailed by the rancher.

"Sheriff, I am missing more stock from my range. When are you going to find those responsible?"

The sheriff walked over to the rancher and replied, "Why, Mr. Elliott, you should've come to me first before telling everyone in town about your lost stock. Are you sure they didn't wander off somewhere on their own?"

Elliott shook his head, "Wakely, you've been Sheriff here for a long time and you've not caught any rustlers, nor the murderer of ole Jesse Sumner for that matter. How you keep your job is beyond me."

Wakely scowled hard at the rancher and advised, "You should keep your opinions to yourself, Elliott," and then, he turned and walked out. The men of the cracker barrel club glared after him.

I thought it time then, so I asked out loud where I could find a job wrangling horses. All eyes were on me and one bewhiskered gent stood up to scrutinize my makeup. His eyes were wise and crafty as he took in the manner in which I wore my gun. He nodded as he pondered me a bit and then, with a grin on his face offered, "Well, Son, if you've a mind to, there's the rocking T ranch about forty miles north of here. Then there's the Cross Bar about 50 miles south of here. But if you are a real good wrangler and a scrapper to boot, then Miss Laura Sumner of the Sumner ranch is looking for good men."

The others took note of what he said and how he said it. I nodded my understanding and asked, "Where can I find this Sumner ranch?" "Easy," he replied, "Take the coach road north for a mile, then when it forks toward the Rockies, take that road for about an hour's ride, you'll see the gates of ole Jesse Sumner's ranch to the right." I thanked him for the information and left. I heard audible murmurs speculating on who I was as I exited the store.

I went to the livery and saddled up Chino. The hostler casually inquired as to where I was headed. He sort of choked up when I told him that I was going to try for a job at the Sumner ranch. Also at that very moment, three rough-looking characters rode past the livery and stopped in front of the sheriff's office. I scrutinized them and was sure that I'd recognized one. "Jake Tanner," I pulled the name from the back of my mind, and he was wanted.

I watched as Tanner entered the jail, then leave a few minutes later. He spoke to his friends and they rode off on the northbound stagecoach road—the same route that I would take to the Sumner ranch. I decided to give them wide berth, and waited about fifteen minutes before leading Chino out of the livery and mounting.

Tanner was reputed to be a real hard hombre without conscience. That he'd killed men before was without question. I had read the flyers on him. Just now, my concern was where were he and his men heading and what was their purpose? That Sheriff Wakley seemed to be in cahoots with them made Judge Wilkerson's surmise all that much more evident. If I was right, they were headed toward the Sumner range and that was bad news for anyone.

As I left town, some folks at the general store stood watching me. They observed me with great interest. I could see in their eyes a wonder of why I was interested in that Sumner spread. Well, they would find out soon enough.

A stagecoach road has many tracks and so it is difficult to say which are which. I took the westward fork as advised by the old man, and as I rode, I thought about how I could best approach Miss Sumner. Riding along and watching for sign, I found where three riders departed the main trail and rode up into the hills. I decided to follow their trail for a bit, on a hunch.

Shortly thereafter, their trail turned northward. I wondered about that. Well, I wasn't getting closer to the Sumner ranch, so I left their trail and turned more westward toward my destination. A few hours later found me sitting lazily on Chino on a grassy knoll overlooking one of the most beautiful ranch yards that I had ever seen. Large shade trees sheltered the rear of the house; an immaculate white porch adorned the front of the house, and would you believe it? A flower garden lined both sides of the front porch.

I was quite taken with the sight of it. I smiled a bit, remembering my mother planting wildflowers around the entrance to our home in West Texas. I touched Chino's side with my spurs and down the hill we went. Riding down towards the front yard, I noticed a thin trail of wood smoke lifting lazily up from where the kitchen ought to be.

Judging by the time of day, I figured that an evening meal was in progress. I thought hard about that beef trail jerky and the cold biscuits that I had been living off for the past hundred miles or so on the way here, and I hoped that Miss Sumner would hire me and spare some good home cooked meals. I rode right up to the front porch, and looked down at that flower garden. I chuckled to myself a mite, then hallowed the house.

A few moments went by before the door opened. Much to my surprise, out walked a beautiful dark-haired young woman. I looked her up and down for a long moment, and I could see right away that she was no ordinary woman. She was dressed in men's denim jeans and blue shirt, and by the way she carried that revolver on her hip, I figured that she sure knew how to use it. I felt silly as I grinned at her.

CHAPTER ELEVEN

The Horsewoman

Laura Sumner rose with the early dawn and dressed for a day of horse hunting in the wilds. After a quick breakfast with coffee, she went to the stables to saddle up Brandy. She spoke softly to the horse and before mounting, paused a long minute for reflective prayer, "Lord, help me find wild horses today. Help me realize my dreams—my destiny." She also thought about her Uncle Jesse, "Help me Jesse, show me where to go."

The young woman then put boot to stirrup and swung into the saddle. Once again, she headed toward the west and the Rockies. Riding alone in the Lower Colorado Territory was dangerous enough for a man accustomed to the wilds, but for a woman; it was shear guts that drove Laura to hunt down the few horses she could find by herself.

After two hours, Laura found tracks of a small bunch of unshod horses. There looked to be about ten in the herd. She turned onto their trail and hurried Brandy along, keeping mindful of the landscape and the horizon. After trailing over several hills, through a forest area, across a creek, and back through more wooded area, she emerged into a long valley. There were the horses, just ahead of her. A small but powerful young black stallion led the group and they were grazing contentedly. The stallion stood watch, periodically sniffing the air for danger.

Laura slowed Brandy to a walk as they carefully approached the herd from the downwind side. They were within fifty yards when the stallion sensed her approach. He looked straight at her for an instant before sounding the alarm. The horses sprang into a dead run with Laura and Brandy hot behind them, shaking out a loop on her lariat.

Laura drove at the stallion, watching him stay behind the herd, performing evasive zigzag movements to hinder his capture. She

75

tracked him closely and, after a long run, finally settled a noose over his neck. The stallion fought the rope, running in a wide arch, then coming straight at Laura and veering at the last moment. Brandy was well trained for this action and countered the stallion's movements.

Painstakingly patient, Laura cautiously reeled him in closer to her. Time passed slowly before Laura had the stallion secured beside her. As she led the stallion toward home, fillies, colts, and foals moved in line with them. Laura smiled a bit while wiping a thankful dusty tear from her eyes. She had succeeded in finding more horses.

Arriving back at the ranch, Laura turned the stallion into the working corral at one end of the stables, and the others she turned into the larger holding corral. After securing the gates, she dismounted Brandy, then climbed the bars of the work corral to watch the black move around for a while.

She loved the way that the horse moved; he was strong, sleek, and full of fire. Laura was invigorated with the prospect of taming this wild creature. This was no sale animal: this horse would be her own personal mount. Names sifted through her mind and she smiled suddenly. "I will call you—*Mickey*. Yes, Mickey it is!" she said under her breath. "Tomorrow you and I shall begin our training."

Being late afternoon, Laura decided to do a quick bathing to rid herself of sweat and dust. A long soak in the galvanized tub in the washroom would be perfect, but that would take several trips for water and time to heat it. Upon second thought, she heated one bucketful, taking it to her room where lavender soap and a washcloth waited. While bathing she envisioned training Mickey and it caused her to smile broadly. Suddenly, she felt hungry, it had been a long time since breakfast. In the excitement of finding and capturing the horses, she had forgotten to eat.

Dressing in fresh Levi's, shirt opened to the second button, and boots, Laura went into the kitchen to prepare slices of beef, potatoes, cobbed corn, and the remaining morning biscuits. Enticing aromas filled the room, as she put on a pot of coffee, strong and black, just like Uncle Jesse liked it. Laura had somewhat acquired the taste for it as well.

The kitchen windows were open to admit the soft cooling breeze. Momentarily, Laura heard a horse whinny. She moved quickly through the living room to stand at the door, watching a lone rider slowly approach the house. She watched him carefully, reading his mannerism. A second thought occurred to her. Heart pounding, Laura ran to the bedroom and grabbed her gunbelt. Returning to the front room, she strapped the Colt Lightning to her waist settling it slightly low, like Uncle Jesse had shown her.

At the door, she flipped open the loading gate, to check the loads, deciding that she was ready for whatever might come. Again, she watched the rider approach. He rode easy on a handsome roan horse with blazed face. The man was tall and slender. He wore rumpled jeans and a faded red shirt underneath a rumpled dark coat. A pale bandana hung loosely around his neck. His lanky frame was topped off by a wide—brimmed dark brown Stetson set back on his head to reveal sandy brown hair. He was unshaven and dusty.

"No doubt a drifter looking for a handout," she thought.

The rider pulled up in front of the house, sitting there for a few moments and pondering her flower garden on each side of the porch. A silly grin spread over his face as he chuckled to himself. Momentarily, the rider's coat was swept back as he moved his right hand around to his side. Laura saw the Colt revolver, the butt of which sat just inches from his hand. This man was no wrangler, nor was he just a plain drifter—he was a gunman.

Just then, the rider called out to the house. She took a deep breath, opened the door, and stepped out to the porch, looking straight into his eyes. They were bright with surprise. She looked deeper—into the soul of his eyes, and suddenly felt a shiver ripple up through her body. Goosebumps appeared on her forearms. She saw gentleness behind the lonely yet smiling eyes. These were not the eyes of a hardened killer.

Laura Sumner looked over the man's lanky frame, sandy-colored hair, and blue-green eyes like she was reading his very soul. His face also held a week's worth of scraggly beard. She paid particular attention to the well-kept Eagle-gripped Colt revolver strapped around his waist and then asked, "This is the Sumner Ranch. What business do you have here?"

His reply was straight forward. Laura watched his eyes closely as he explained, "I'm sort of down on my luck right now and back there at Miller's Station, I heard talk of you needing good horse wranglers. Well, I've done some horse taming in recent years and thought that I would ride on out here to ask for a job."

Again Laura studied the manner in which he wore the Colt. This man knew something about guns. She didn't know why, but she felt an unexplainable liking for this stranger. She was careful with her next question as many a Western man had forsaken his own name from eastern parts and assumed a different name for a new identity. "How are you called—what's your name?"

The man's answer again came fluidly, "Cole—Bob Cole." In the back of his mind, he had not lied about it. He was christened Robert Cole Stockton. He continued, "I helped break horses for my father's spread and also wrangled for a ranch in the New Mexico Territory. I even joined a cattle drive to Abilene, Kansas." He didn't mention that he wasn't the wrangler on the drive.

His experience sounded good enough for Laura. Instinctively she was ready to hire this man. Her intellect told her to secure his services in a different capacity, namely his prowess with a gun. She would explain it to him over supper. "Alright, Bob Cole, I'll give you a try. Stable your horse and take your gear to the bunkhouse. It's empty, so you can take your pick of the bunks. Wash up and come back here to the house. I've got supper already started. I'll set you a place, and we'll talk further."

Cole Stockton, now known to Laura Sumner as Bob Cole, thanked her for the opportunity and rode over to the stable. Stripping his gear, then stabling Chino, he looked over the others in the building. The animals were good sturdy stock. He appraised those in the holding corral—a young bunch. Then, he saw the young black stallion in the working corral. That was a good horse. All in all, he saw potential for this operation, if only she had some men to do the work.

Cole carried his saddlebags, bedroll, Winchester, and tote to the bunkhouse. The building was constructed of hewn logs locked together, along with a river-mud-clay based mortar to seal the crevices. Once inside, he looked around. It was like every other bunkhouse that he had seen.

Five bunks lined the walls around a small wooden table and straight-backed chairs. There was an oil lamp in the middle of the table along with a candle set in a metal holder and a box of sulfur matches. A deck of playing cards sat in disarray to one side of the table. Pegs were driven into the walls for hanging equipment. A potbellied stove stood at the far end of the open room with a box of kindling next to it. An earthen water jug hung in netted hemp from the ceiling with a wooden ladle attached to it. Faded blue linen curtains dressed the two windows. Cole chose a window bunk and opened both windows to air out the musty odor.

Out back of the quarters he found a rain barrel half full of water and a stand with basin, soap, and towel. A small mirror hung on the outside wall, and as he surveyed his reflection, mused that he could sure use a shave. He would do that in the morning.

After washing his face and hands as well as dusting himself off a mite, Cole wandered over towards the house, taking in the scenery along the way. The ranch was well situated with a creek in close proximity. Firewood was abundant, and there was a small vegetable garden to the side of the house.

Looking toward the west, Cole watched the position of the sun against the Rockies. It would be dark soon. As he neared the house, the aroma of supper met him. He could swear that there was beef simmering, biscuits baking, and coffee brewing. Stepping up on the porch, he thought to knock at the door. Within moments, Laura appeared and opened the door. Smiling, she beckoned him to the kitchen. "Help yourself to coffee," she said. "Go and sit on the porch. Supper will keep. I like to watch the sunset from the porch. I'll join you in a few minutes."

Cole took down two blue cups from the cupboard and filled each. Taking his cup, he went to the porch as requested and sat in a wooden armchair, sipping the strong brew. Laura was right, the scene before them was exhilarating—a spectrum of gold to red rays formed a background behind the dark blue of the Rocky Mountains, the land before it turning purple and then indistinguishable in darkness. Laura momentarily joined him. "This is always my favorite time of day," she said reflectively. "Uncle Jesse and I would sit out here and watch the sunset every evening. I do miss him." After the sun disappeared beyond the mountaintops, Laura rose and said, "Come, supper is ready. I hope you like beef, potatoes, and biscuits." To Cole, that was the call to a feast of home cooking at its best.

When they entered the kitchen area, Laura lit an oil lamp hanging from the ceiling. Cole poured more coffee and lit the large candle on the table for a bit more light. Laura motioned him to a chair across the table from her. As he sat down, she filled a blue plate with several thick slices of beef, potatoes, gravy, and corn on the cob. There was butter and a berry jam on the table near a combination salt and pepper cellar. Filling her own plate, she joined him, placing a plate of biscuits between them. Their eyes met for a long minute before either of them spoke.

Cole opened the conversation, "I've looked over your place here, and I see potential. The stock seems solid and the location is good."

Laura looked thoughtful before she replied, "Mr. Cole—Bob, you seem to know ranch layout pretty well. I inherited this ranch and all its holdings from my late Uncle Jesse. He built this spread. About three months ago, the rustling began. As I understand it, my uncle must've trailed and found the rustlers with his stock. He was killed where he found them. I inquired of the sheriff as to what has been done to find his killers, but he claims to have found no one. He told me that those responsible were probably passersby long gone from this area. They most likely went to Mexico with the stock."

Laura paused a moment to sip coffee before continuing, "Other ranches are also missing stock. I believe that Sheriff Jack Wakely lied to me. I believe that the murderers are still here and he knows who they are. I wrote the U.S. Marshal in Denver asking for an investigation, but as of yet, I have not heard nor seen a thing from them. Maybe no one else cares, but I do. I want to find those responsible for Jesse's death and I want to see them answer for it."

Cole leaned forward in the chair, cocking his head a bit to one side. He was highly interested in what Laura related.

She further confided, "As for this ranch, I've been advised in so many words that it would be best that I leave this area and forget about it. I assure you, I am not leaving. I am going to build this ranch into something to be proud of—a ranch that produces the best horses in the territory. That's what I am going to do."

Cole nodded his understanding while Laura continued, "When I arrived, there were five wranglers working here. One left because he wouldn't work for a woman, one was killed in a wild horse accident, and the other three deserted me in the middle of the night. I need good men in order to meet the deadlines to pay a bank loan and other debts. I can't pay much until I sell a lot of horses. I just wanted you to understand the situation here before you decide to stay." Under her breath, she softly whispered, "and I hope you do stay."

Cole looked her straight in the eyes and nodded affirmatively, "I will stay and work this with you. What would you have me do?"

Laura took a long minute before replying, "This brings us to the job that I have in mind for you." She took a deep breath, "I can say that you are a good horseman and a lover of horses because the care that you give your horse shows. But, your hands tell a different story. You are no wrangler, at least not recently. The Colt in your well-worn holster shows definite care and by the way you wear your gunbelt, you know about guns and how to use them. I imagine that you have another one on you somewhere close. Men like you usually do."

Cole thought, "She told it pretty well right. I usually carry my second Colt in the back of my belt, out of sight."

Laura spoke further, "You don't look like an outlaw, so I would say that you are probably on the verge of the law. I want to hire you to ride watch on my ranch and stock. I want you to catch the one or ones responsible for the rustling, and quite possibly, the person responsible for my uncle's death. Well, there it is, Bob Cole. That is what I have in mind. Are you up to that?"

Cole Stockton lowered his gaze for a few moments to collect his thoughts, "There it is. She laid it out for me. She wants a range detective of sorts and that's just the ticket that I need. By the way, just how does an outlaw look? Not all are obvious. Well, I can't turn it down under the circumstances." Cole again met Laura's eyes, "Yes, Miss Sumner. I believe I can handle that type of work. How much is the job worth?"

Laura did some mental calculations before announcing, "Right now, I can pay only fifty dollars for the whole month. Will you accept the job?"

Cole grinned a silly grin and said, "Fifty dollars a month is fine, that is, if you will throw in a few of these meals as well. And, I'll even help with the stock for the time being. Maybe together, we can get something going here."

Laura was taken with his candidness and his silly smile. It resembled a little boy caught with his hand in the cookie jar. "You are hired," Laura said. "We start early here. I will see you for breakfast just past sunrise."

Taking the hint, Cole stood, finished off his coffee, then bid his good evening before sauntering off to the bunkhouse. As he crossed the ranch yard, he had the feeling that he was being watched. At the bunkhouse, he sat down on the bench just outside the door and pulled the tobacco makings from the inside pocket of his coat, his fingers momentarily brushing against the silver star hidden there.

He rolled a smoke and lit it with a sulfur match. Taking a long draw on the homemade smoke, Cole thought about this ranch, Laura Sumner's assessment of the situation and her thoughts about the sheriff. He thought of the woman herself. She was a beautiful woman, and she could cook. Not only could she cook, she could handle guns, of that he was sure. He would get a good night's rest before planning his next move.

Cole stood, ground the cigarette out in the dirt with the toe of his boot, and entered the bunkhouse. It was pitch dark as he felt his way to the table. Striking a match, he lit the solitary candle and stood there a moment watching eerie, flickering shadows dance back and forth on the walls.

He pondered the day's events as he undressed for bed. Laura Sumner's evaluation of Sheriff Jack Wakley seemed to coincide with his own observations, not to mention the rancher Elliott's confrontation with Wakley. Judge Wilkerson's initial estimation of the man seemed to hold substance. There was certainly something sinister going on around Miller's Station. Time usually tells all, and Cole Stockton knew then that he was hot on the trail of discovery.

He stretched a bit, yawned, then blew out the candle and lay down. As he slept, he dreamed about this woman, Laura Sumner. There was something about her, something that wouldn't let him go, something that pulled at his mind and his heart.

CHAPTER TWELVE

Riding The Wild Whirlwind

The sun's early morning rays were just peeking over the eastern land when Laura Sumner awoke. She lay still for a few minutes letting her eyes adjust to the dimness of the room before stretching out her body. Afterward, she languished for a while longer as she pondered the day's plans. Today, she was going to work with Mickey, her new mount. Only then, did she remember that Bob Cole was in the bunkhouse and would probably be rising shortly. She must get dressed and prepare breakfast for the two of them.

Rising from her bed and shedding her night clothes, Laura moved to the wash basin and pitcher of water. She poured the basin half full, then took her washcloth and soap to bathe herself. Afterwards, she dressed in her Levi's, boots, and linen shirt.

Laura tied her hair with a dark ribbon before moving to the kitchen to fire up the iron wood stove. While the fire was catching, she ground coffee beans, then set the coffee pot on the stove to boil. She decided on corn meal hot cakes with molasses and bacon for the meal so set about mixing the batter.

Every so often she peered out the kitchen window to see if her new hired hand was up and about. A comfortable feeling filled her when she observed Bob Cole leave the bunkhouse and go directly to the stables. Here was a man who cared for his animals before himself. Laura hummed a tune as she continued preparing the breakfast.

*   *   *

Cole Stockton rose with the first rays of the sun peeking through a window and stripped to the waist. Taking up his shaving mug, brush, and razor, he stepped through the back door of the bunkhouse to the porcelain basin to wash up. He lathered up his week-old whiskers and using the leather strap hanging by the basin, stropped his razor a few times to sharpen it. He touched the edge lightly and found it satisfactory. A shave with cold water isn't too comfortable, but it felt good to him. Afterward, he dressed in a clean blue linen shirt. Then he slung his gunbelt around his slim waist and stepped into the ranch yard.

The aroma of freshly-brewed coffee and bacon frying stimulated his senses as he walked to the stables. He would see to the stock before breakfast. He pitched hay into all of the feeders and also laid in a bait of grain to each. Next came fresh water to each stall. Afterward, he walked to the front porch where he knocked and stood waiting for Laura to bid him enter.

Cole didn't have to wait long. The beautiful young woman smiled when she saw him clean shaven. She found him most handsome. During the meal Laura outlined her plans for the day. She would work Mickey, the new stallion. "I might need some help with the black. Would you help me?" she inquired.

"Certainly," he replied. "If you want, I'll do the chore for you."

Laura thought for moment before replying, "No, Bob. That stallion is going to be my personal mount from now on and I must do this myself. However, I'd feel a lot better knowing that you are watching out for me." He nodded his concurrence.

After the meal Cole waited on the porch with a cup of coffee while Laura got herself ready for the wild ride they both knew was coming. She donned her chaps and spurs, pulled on her waist length denim jacket, grabbed up her lucky black Stetson. Only then, did the two of them walk to the stables.

Laura picked up her saddle and blanket along with a hackamore bridle and reins. Cole found a braided lariat and together they moved to the work corral. He stepped inside the corral to have the black grow instantly wary of him. The horse pranced around, moving quickly back and forth, then breaking into a run straight at him. The horse then suddenly veered away, running around the corral.

Cole moved with the horse, shaking out a loop to swing it around his head. The loop sailed through the air and expertly settled around the black's neck. Cole dashed to the center post and looped the lariat around it pulling hard. The black came straight at him in an attempt to run him down, but Cole moved quickly. As the horse got closer, he pulled in the slack until the horse was finally at the post. Cole now spoke softly to the horse, stroking him gently until the animal settled down.

Laura entered the corral with her gear as Cole slipped the hackamore onto the black's head. He pulled off his bandana and tied it with a slipknot over the animal's eyes before slipping the lariat off. Cole held the horse by the halter while Laura eased on the blanket and then settled the saddle in place on his back. The horse quivered with the weight of the saddle and Laura spoke to it. She stroked his sleek neck and talked to Mickey as if she were already his master. Finally, the black again settled down and she was able to tighten the cinches. The horse was ready.

Laura took a deep breath, exhaled, and then placed boot to stirrup and up into the saddle she went. The black shook with excitement as the never-before-felt weight settled onto his back. Laura took up the reins and nodded to Cole. He pulled the blind from the horse's face. A moment went by before the black suddenly sprang into action.

Cole moved back to the corral bars to watch this woman in earnest. He couldn't help thinking that some women were better at breaking horses than men. His mother had also broken horses for his father.

Laura was game all the way and for some reason, he felt proud of her. The stallion jumped forward with his hind legs shooting straight into the air as Laura sailed up with him. The jolt back to earth was bone-rattling and teeth jarring, but Laura stuck with him. Around and around the corral they moved—hopping, jumping, twisting, and crashing down.

Suddenly the black sprang into a wild twisting movement and Laura sailed into the air coming down to earth with a dusty thud. Cole started toward her, but she quickly rose only to wave him off. The horse ran around the corral for a bit, then stood looking at Laura from the far end of the enclosure.

Laura moved to Mickey speaking soothingly. The black stood still until she was at his side. He let her gather up the reins and put foot to stirrup before the game of "who—flung—the—chunk?" began again.

Several minutes later Laura once again stirred up the dust with her body. She glanced at Bob Cole who was watching intently.

Again, she waved him off and proceeded to remount. "This time will be different," she thought as she mentally calculated the horse's movements. "This time I'll be ready for him."

The black waited for her to mount. He now understood this *game* and he was ready to continue. Laura sided the animal again, speaking softly. Her shirt was streaked with sweat, her face was dirty, and every muscle of her body ached. Laura set her jaw in steadfast determination and climbed back into the saddle.

The horse did a spiral movement, but she was ready for it and hung on tightly. Around and around the corral they fought each other. Seconds turned into minutes and the minutes ticked by slowly as the choking dust and sweat from the wild whirlwind of woman and beast churned in the air and fell as waves to the ground.

The black was slowing now, and Laura felt it. She was winning this struggle of mind over muscle. A few more minutes of light bucking transitioned into a walk around the corral with Laura proudly guiding the animal through various maneuvers. She finally rode Mickey to the corral gate and sat him looking into the smiling eyes of a widely grinning Cole.

Laura dismounted Mickey and spent the next few minutes stroking and speaking to the animal. She repeated his name several times and the black seemed to understand. Afterward, the three of them walked to the stable where Laura unsaddled Mickey and led him to a special stall. There, she rubbed him down with fresh straw while he drank cool water from a bucket and munched fresh hay and grain from the feed box. Cole stood silently watching her with admiration.

Afterward, Cole and Laura walked back to the house. They talked as they walked and he suggested that in the morrow, she show him the ranch.

"If I am to do the job you asked, I should know the territory to protect. Besides, there might just be some overlooked clues in the area that could help us find the rustlers and those responsible for Jesse's death," said Cole.

"That's a good idea, Bob. It will be good for Mickey also, to be ridden the bounds of this ranch. I can continue his training while we ride."

Laura prepared a quick supper of beef stew with potatoes and vegetables. They talked as they ate and Laura once again spoke of her plans for the ranch. Tonight she included her idea to breed the strongest horses and to train them gently for sale. Cole commented that he heard tell how some Indians trained their best warhorses in a gentle manner.

Laura turned the conversation to her family. She told of her parents' farm in Dallas and of Uncle Jesse's visit that inspired her to learn of horses. Then, she asked a critical question, "Do you have family, Bob?"

He thought a moment before replying, "Yes, my parents have a small spread in West Texas along the Comanche Trace. I was raised there doing the same chores that you did. I was taught about guns, hunting, and fishing. I have a younger brother, Clay, who is a much better hunter than me." Laura's interest perked with his story about his early life. At last, Laura suggested that they retire to get a good night's sleep as the next day would be busy.

It was well after dark when Cole returned to the bunkhouse and readied himself for bed. Laura was on his mind and the more he thought of her, the more he liked her.

Laura also readied herself for bed and she, likewise, thought of this man Bob Cole. She liked his easy mannerism. Hearing of his background helped Laura know and appreciate this man. She smiled inwardly as she recounted the day. She fell asleep satisfied that she had tamed her new mount, Mickey. Laura believed she had found a good friend in Bob Cole.

*   *   *

It was just after midnight when Cole awakened with muffled sounds coming from the stable. He listened intently and heard it again. The horses were snorting and milling uneasily around the corral. He rose quickly and pulled on his jeans and boots. He grabbed his gunbelt and strapped it on as he moved to the door. Drawing his Colt, he cracked open the door of the bunkhouse and peered into the darkness. Letting his eyes adjust to the moonlit outdoors, he eased out to the end of the log building where he backed into the shadows to wait.

A minute or so ticked by before he saw the door of the stable swing wide open. There were three figures, one afoot and two were mounted. They were trying to shoo the horses out of the stable and adjoining corral. Horses whinnied and bucked while the three men waved their arms wildly. Midnight rustling was in progress.

Cole stepped out of the shadows and yelled, "Let them horses be!" and at the same time leveled his Colt at one of the mounted men. Orange stabs of flame were their reply as bullets whined past his person. He shot the man, watching him jerk out of the saddle to hit the ground stiffly. He then turned his revolver to the second mounted man who jerked his horse around and rode, firing his revolver at the dark shadow across the yard. Cole took careful aim and shot this man out of the saddle, too.

The outlaw hit the ground with a hard thud, rolled a few feet, and never moved again. The third man had grabbed his horse, mounted, and fired rapidly at Cole as he rode past the house. Bullets smacked into the logs behind him. Suddenly, a loud boom of buckshot emptied his saddle and he lay grotesque and twisted in death.

Laura Sumner, barefoot in a white nightgown and wielding a shotgun, stepped cautiously off the porch.

Cole moved to the man downed near the corral first, knelt, and looked down on the dying man's face. "You're dying," he said. "There's nothing I can do for you. Make your *Peace*. Who sent you? When the man hesitated, Cole leaned closer to him and raised his voice, "Dammit, answer me! Who do you work for?"

The man shivered and coughed hard. Blood oozed from his mouth. With gravelly voice the man admitted, "Jack Wakely sent us to take the stock. He's the boss. Who are you?"

Cole answered the man truthfully, "Cole Stockton, U.S. Marshal." And, then the fallen man retched out another hard bloody cough and passed to the *Almighty*.

Laura approached Cole and the dead man, "Did he say anything? Who sent them?"

Cole shook his head negatively, "No, Miss Sumner, he didn't say anything understandable. You go and try to get some rest. I'll take care of the dead. Tomorrow, I'll take them into town to the Sheriff for burial."

Laura nodded her understanding and turned back to the house. On her mind was the sight of Bob Cole standing steady against those three men. But, even more so on her mind was the burning question of, "What would have happened if I were alone here? Thank God for Bob Cole."

Chapter Thirteen

Showdown At Miller's Station

At first light, Cole hitched up the ranch wagon and loaded the three bodies into it. He studied the brands on the horses of the fallen men and correctly surmised them to be stolen stock. He decided to leave the horses with Laura for the time being.

Laura had a quick breakfast ready when he finished loading the dead into the wagon. He appraised her of his plan over breakfast, "I will deliver these dead to Sheriff Wakely with explanations of their demise. I should return in a few hours."

Before climbing to the wagon seat, Cole returned to the bunkhouse and filled his belt with cartridges, checked the loads in his holstered Colt, then got his second revolver from his saddlebags. He loaded the second revolver as well and stuck it out of sight in the back of his belt.

When he left, Laura was standing on the bottom step of the porch and called out, "Hurry back, Bob Cole."

He gave her a quick smile and wave as he slapped reins to the team. Laura watched him drive out of sight toward Miller's Station. She took a deep breath and exhaled. The thought clung to her mind, "I like this man. I hope he stays a while. I'd like to know him better."

The trip to Miller's Station was slow, but it gave Cole the time to plan a course of action. He would leave the team at the livery with the dead intact. Then he would go to the sheriff's office to arrest Jack Wakley and all deputies with him. That there would be gunplay was without question. Cole steeled himself for the task at hand, thinking "Justice is coming to Miller's Station today and may the devil take the hindmost."

Just over an hour later, Cole halted the team in front of the livery stable. The hostler stepped out to meet him and after peering in the back of the wagon remarked, "Holy mackerel! What happened to them?"

Cole replied, "They ran into something they couldn't handle. Watch this wagon for me. I'll be back to make arrangements in a short while." The hostler nodded his understanding as Cole Stockton walked with determination toward the jail.

*   *   *

I took my time walking the distance to the jail, taking care to identify any deputy that I might run across. I hoped that Wakely would be by himself, but it really didn't matter to me how many were with him. I held the element of surprise and was ready for any number of them. Just for good measure, I touched the butt of my holstered Colt and lifted it slightly to loosen it.

Upon arrival at the jail, I opened the door and stepped in. Wakely was not alone. Two deputies were standing near his side with cups of coffee in their hands. Wakely looked up, an agitated look spread across his face. He sensed that I was not there to pass the time of day, so stood quickly. "Just who the hell are you and what do you want here?" he growled.

I just blurted it out, "Wakely, I just brought in three dead men from the Sumner ranch. You and your deputies are under arrest for rustling and murder."

He was quick to snap back, "By whose authority?" as he reached for his revolver. In fact, all three went for their guns.

"Samuel Colt," I retorted with my own Colt in hand. All three faces turned ashen. I shot Wakley in the center of his body which caused him to stagger back against the wall while attempting to bear his own gun on me. I turned and methodically shot each of the other deputies twice before turning back to Wakley. Deputy Forgy was dead before he hit the floor. The other lay wounded in the corner, his pistol out of reach.

"You shot me!" Wakley exclaimed, "Just who the hell are you?"

"Cole Stockton, United States Marshal," I replied as I drew my second Colt from the back of my belt and also leveled it at him. He didn't answer me. He dropped his gun and fell back against the wall breathing heavily.

I heard shouts and commotion coming closer to the jail and was quite sure that the other three deputies were almost upon me. I quickly grabbed a shotgun from the gun rack and moved to behind the potbellied stove. The door swung open and two men rushed inside, guns at the ready. "Drop those guns and grab sky!" I ordered.

Both men fired at me, their first bullets clinking into the stove. I raised up and fired both barrels at once. One deputy slammed back against the stone wall while the second was blown back through the door to lie bloody in the street. The third man failed to enter and I went cautiously through the door after him.

I found him across the street at a hitching rack grabbing frantically for a skittish horse that kept shying away from him. I walked steadily toward him yelling, "U.S. Marshal, drop your gun and surrender!"

He turned and fired at me. The bullet whizzed past me to smack into the stone jail. I immediately shot him. He recoiled for a moment and fired at me once more. I stepped toward him, shooting him again and again, until he dropped the pistol and slumped to the ground. I walked carefully up to the man and checked his breathing. I found him dead. I reached down to rip the authoritative star from his shirtfront and put it in my coat pocket.

Townspeople began to crowd forward as I retrieved and pinned on my own star. People looked at me with wondering eyes. I noticed a man from the general store looking at my badge, nodding his head, as though he had already guessed my purpose a few days ago. I turned to the crowd and said, "Someone get the doctor and the undertaker to come. I've got business for both."

I went back to Wakely. He was out cold on the jail floor. From him, as well as well as each deputy, I ripped the stars off their shirts and jackets. I picked up all their guns and stacked them on the desk. Then, I grabbed Wakley by the feet and dragged him to an empty cell where I left him lying on the hard floor. I got the wounded deputy and did likewise. Curious townspeople stared in through the door and windows.

Finally, I turned to two other prisoners locked up to learn why they were in jail. The first was drunk and disorderly. I let him out and told him to go home. The second was a vagrant, and I released him also. I suggested that he see the hostler at the livery for a job. I locked the door to Wakely and the deputy's cell. They would stand trial in Judge Wilkerson's Court.

When the undertaker arrived, I appraised him of the dead inside the jail and in the street. He rounded up some men to gather up the dead and carry them over to his place of business. "By the way," I added, "did I tell you that there's three more dead in a wagon at the livery? Get them, too."

Yet another man entered the jail and before I could speak, he called out quietly, "Marshal, I am Doctor Simmons. Where are the wounded? Everyone I see from here are dead." I pointed him through the center door to the cells, "There are two locked up back there Doc." I escorted him back to the cells where Wakely and the other deputy were locked up, then left him to do his work.

At that moment, two of the ole boys from the general store bunch entered the jail. They had come to tell me something strange was going on at the bank. "What kind of strange doings?" I asked.

One replied, "The banker just gave his two tellers the rest of the day off and now the shades are down. The doors are locked. The Closed sign is in the door window."

Now, that really sounded suspicious to me. To one, I asked, "What's your name?" "Roberts," he replied. I reached into my coat pocket to get a deputy badge, pinned it on his vest and said, "You are now, Deputy Roberts." I reached to the desk and gave him a revolver. As his eyes widened, I said, "You keep people away from here until I get back."

To the other, I asked the same question. "Johnson," came his answer. I pinned a star on him also. "Johnson, you come with me. I want you to point out the banker when we find him."

We went out into the street where Johnson surveyed the crowd, "He's not here."

I addressed the townspeople, "Has anyone seen the banker?"

One man stepped forward and related, "He lives just one street over behind this street. He keeps a buggy and horse there."

Johnson and I hurried toward his house. The crowd followed us. Just as we turned the corner, Banker Smith climbed into his one-horse buggy ready to give whip to the chestnut mare.

I drew my Colt and issued the challenge, "U.S. Marshal! Smith, you run, I'll shoot you. Drop that whip and get out of that buggy!" He took the better way. With defeat on his face, he dropped the whip to the floor of the buggy. He sat with his hands in the air.

I made it to the man's side where I reached for the black satchel on the seat beside him. I opened it and peered inside. The bag held a good part of the townfolk's savings, in cash and other negotiable instruments. I advised Smith that he was under arrest for thievery and other charges were pending as I unraveled the doings. In an effort to save his neck, Smith rattled off, "It was Wakely who killed Jesse Sumner! I had nothing to do with that!"

Now the puzzle began coming together. Jack Wakely was the muscle and Julius Smith was the brains behind the rustling ring. Smith would make loans to the people while Wakely and company would steal them blind. Next, Smith would force a foreclosure so that all property belonged to the thieves. They needed a secluded ranch to move stolen stock. Jesse Sumner's place fit the bill. It was remote, yet on the way from the Colorado Territory passes into the New Mexico Territory where they sold the stolen stock.

I reached into the wagon to grab Smith and jerked him to the ground. His legs were wobbly as I spun him around and pointed him toward the jail. With the satchel in one hand, I took the scruff of Smith's neck in the other. Escorted by dozens of townspeople, Johnson and I marched him to the jail where we locked him up for safekeeping.

Then, I dispersed the crowd telling them, "Justice has come to Miller's Station, and these men will face Judge Wilkerson's court as soon as I can get them there."

I got the feeling that they would liked to have strung them up; however, the crowd left and I settled down to sort through my next steps. I deputized two more townspeople to guard the jail overnight. I had to return to the Sumner Ranch for my belongings as well as explain to Laura the outcome of her letter to the United States Marshal.

*   *   *

It was early afternoon, when Sam Evans, a rider from the neighboring Cross Bar T ranch visited the Sumner ranch to pass on the news. He began, "There was an all out, hell-to-pay gunfight in the middle of town at the jail. Sheriff Wakley and one deputy were wounded. Four other deputies, including George Forgy, are dead. Julius Smith, the banker, was arrested by the Deputy United States Marshal as he tried to leave town. He's got them all in jail now."

"A Deputy United States Marshal?" Laura asked with quivering voice.

"Yah, name's Cole Stockton. It was a sight to see, all right—Stockton walked right into the jail, and told the sheriff and his deputies they were under arrest. Well, Wakley and his boys thought that they could shoot faster and then the ball opened. Stockton shot hell out Of them in the jail, then walked outside and got the sixth man. Miss Sumner, I've got to get to my boss now and tell him the news."

Laura thanked the man for the information before she sat on the porch step in disbelief. Suddenly, a realization of Bob Cole's real identity dawned. The man she had become more than fond of so quickly must be none other than the well-known Cole Stockton. He was reputed to be one of the best gunfighters in the Territory.

Uncle Jesse's words again flooded her mind, "Sometimes a man is not what he appears to be."

Cole Stockton was not as she had envisioned him. She had looked deep into the eyes of his soul, and saw loneliness and a longing; yet also, she saw gentleness and a man of honor.

Then Maude Pritchard's tealeaf prediction hit her like a bolt of lightning, "One will stoke the fires of your soul. He is born of deadly skill, but you will seek the comfort of his honor."

Laura Lynne Sumner blushed at herself. She hardly knew this man, Cole Stockton, yet she found that she was taken with his easy honest manner and silly grin. Could Cole Stockton be the man foretold in her destiny? She swallowed hard. She could certainly love such a man.

Her next thought showed her feminine side. "He's only seen me in working clothes and probably feels that I am too much of a wrangler to notice me for what I really am. I must change because he will be stopping back to pick up his things. I want him to know that I am a woman first." She went into the house to clean up and change clothes. She wanted to prepare a supper for them to share.

Within a couple of hours a thick beef and vegetable stew simmered on the stove. Biscuits were baked and still warm in the pan. Fresh coffee was ready for pouring. Laura sat on the porch dressed in a flowered print dress that enhanced her figure. She anxiously watched the trail to town.

It was near dusk when she saw him coming. Goosebumps rose on her arms and a quiver ran up her spine. Her heart skipped a beat as he reined in at the hitching post. The last rays of sunlight glinted off metal pinned to his shirtfront. Laura recognized it. It was the silver star of a Deputy United States Marshal.

Cole Stockton looked down at her and a wide grin spread over his face. His eyes shined bright with anticipation. He dismounted and rounded the roan. Laura beamed with the radiance of life itself. The two of them gazed deeply into one another's eyes. Instant communication passed between them.

"Cole Stockton," she began, "I knew that you were no wrangler or outlaw. I sense these things, and am usually right. Why didn't you tell me who you were?"

"It was Judge Wilkerson's idea and I couldn't take the chance of being found out before I got the evidence I needed. I'm sorry, but I just couldn't tell you," Cole replied. He continued, "Tomorrow, I will be escorting my prisoners to Denver for trial. Rest assured that Jack Wakely and company will answer for Jesse's murder as well as all the rustling in this area."

Laura nodded her understanding. "I have supper on the stove," she said. "Wash up. We can talk while we eat." Cole turned to go to the bunkhouse. "Mr. Stockton—Cole, you can wash up here, if you'd like." He followed her into the house and caught the scent of lavender as she preceded him.

They visited over supper and she asked about his travels. "Do you think that you'll be back this way soon—I mean do you travel this way often?"

He replied that he traveled wherever the job took him and that it was possible for him to visit sometime.

Laura smiled and said, "I'd like that, Cole. I'd like that a lot."

It was late when Cole walked over to the bunkhouse for a few hours sleep. He knew that she would have a breakfast waiting for him in the morning before he left the ranch. Cole thought of events in his life before falling sleep that night.

He thought of the well over two dozen vicious gunfights that he'd been part of. He thought of his loneliness on the wild trails that he rode. He thought, "Could a woman like Laura love a man like me? I'm a man known to the gun—a man seemingly born to kill." The term *gunfighter* came to mind, and he shuddered at that thought.

The next morning, Cole was up early and had his gear packed. He led Chino to the house where Laura met him at the door. She had biscuits and bacon with fresh coffee prepared. After a visit, Laura walked out to his horse with him. Before he mounted, he held his hand out to her, "Laura, I meet a lot of people in my travels. If I meet some good horse-savvy men, I'll send them your way."

"I'd like that, Cole. You take care—and come back soon. I'd like to see you again."

When their hands touched, each felt the fire of the other's soul. Cole looked into Laura's eyes and a gentle peace filled his being. Her touch was a softness that he had never felt before.

Cole turned and mounted, taking a last look at the beautiful horsewoman before touching Chino's flanks with his spurs. It was then that he sensed it—he was destined to become an integral part of this woman's life.

A gentle mist filled Laura's eyes as Cole Stockton rode out the gates toward Miller's Station. Once again, Maude's prediction floated across Laura's mind, "One will stoke the fires of your soul." Laura Lynn Sumner knew then, deep in her heart, that he would come back to her. This was her destiny.

CHAPTER FOURTEEN

Stagecoach To Denver

An hour after leaving the Sumner ranch, I entered town and rode directly to the jail. My special deputies were making ready for me to take the prisoners. I walked to the stagecoach depot to inquire about the scheduled coach to Denver. The station manager advised that the coach would be on time. No regular passengers would be allowed on this trip. There would be only my three prisoners with two special deputies inside the coach. The driver and one shotgun guard would ride the box, and I would ride beside the coach on Chino.

Checking the schedule, I learned that the trip to Denver would take us three days. That included a change of teams every twenty to twenty-five miles. I couldn't help but think, "A lot could happen in three days."

When I returned to the jail, Doctor Simmons was there to examine the two wounded prisoners. He verified that both were able to travel. He also provided a packet of extra dressings just in case they were needed.

At the designated time, the coach with six-horse team was standing in front of the stagecoach depot. Townspeople gathered along the street to watch justice in action. A few minutes later, my two special deputies and I escorted a very haggard looking, handcuffed trio to the coach and boarded them sitting side by side on the rear-most seat. The two deputies boarded and sat just under the driver's seat, facing the three prisoners. Each was armed with revolvers for short range.

Within minutes, the burly driver and stern-looking shotgun messenger climbed to the box seat and situated themselves. The driver looked down at me questioningly so I nodded.

"Hang on, boys, here we go!" the driver shouted, and in the next instant, with the snap of his long whip above the team's heads and "Y-o-o-o, team! Hee-haw! Lead them out now, Jubal!"

The coach lurched forward as the team surged into the harnesses, and down Main Street we went heading north. The coach rocked and swayed in the well-traveled ruts. The wounded men moaned at first with the rough ride, but fell silent as they accustomed to the rocking of the coach. About a half mile outside of town, the coach slowed to its regular travel speed. That was the way of it. Some coach drivers liked to put on a show of flurry when leaving or entering a station, but the time in between was paced to preserve the stamina of the animals. Just now, the team was clip-clopping along at an easy, synchronized trot.

Twenty or so miles later, we pulled into the first swing station to change teams, and I saw that the hostlers already had the fresh team hitched up and waiting. I also noticed four saddled horses tied at the corral and grew suspicious. The coach ground to a halt in front of the stationhouse and I dismounted on the far side of it. I stepped to the front-most window of the coach on the outer side and advised the two deputies to be wary. I looked straight at Jack Wakely and he glared back at me.

A few moments later, Jake Tanner and his two henchmen stepped out of the shadows of the stationhouse. I had almost forgotten about them. All three had revolvers in hand, and Tanner blurted out to the shotgun guard, "Drop that shotgun and raise your hands."

They hadn't seen me yet. My Colt was out and ready when I rounded the coach. I shot Tanner in the chest and turned my gun on the leftmost outlaw when the express guard fired, killing the one on the right. A shot from inside the coach took the left standing man before I could pull the trigger. My inside deputies were alert.

I glanced inside the coach again to see that my second deputy had all three prisoners covered with his handgun. Wakley's face was ashen with disbelief. He had counted on making his escape through Tanner's efforts. Now, I could cross one more desperado off Judge Wilkerson's list.

I stepped inside the building to find the stationmaster and two others gagged and hogtied. Tanner's bunch had to let the hostlers harness the waiting team in order to make it appear that all was well.

When the shooting began, the hostlers quickly ducked and hid, not peering out until the firing ceased.

Some twenty minutes later, the coach pulled out again, a bit behind schedule, but still in charge of its consignment. The stationmaster and his folks took charge of the dead and their belongings. Chino and I again trotted beside the coach as we continued northward to Denver and the judge's reckoning.

Just after dusk we pulled into the plaza at Pueblo, Colorado Territory. We jailed our three prisoners with the town marshal and his deputies for safekeeping along with a warning to stay alert and not let anyone except us into the jail.

After seeing to Chino in the stagecoach stables, Deputies Smith, Jacobs, and I stepped out to take stock of the town. Glancing around the plaza, we located a cantina for supper. For an extra fifty cents apiece we had a place to lay our heads for the night. Somewhere on the plaza, the soft strumming of a guitar lent a soothing finale to our first day of travel.

*   *   *

The next morning I stepped out back of the cantina to a washstand where I found a small pump beside a basin. A bar of homemade soap and a stack of laundered flour sack towels were also handy. The water was refreshingly cool and I languished in it, taking my time washing up for breakfast.

Several minutes later, I joined Smith and Jacobs at a table in the back of the dining area. Breakfast was served by a young woman of about seventeen years. We ate heartily of eggs, potatoes, bacon, biscuits, and coffee. There was locally collected honey that we spooned copiously onto our biscuits.

The plaza outside the cantina soon came alive with the bustling of merchants and tradesmen setting up shop for the day. The jingling of trace chains amid snorting and stamping of horses from across the plaza alerted me that the coach was being readied for departure. I finished my coffee and left the deputies to saddle up Chino.

As I readied Chino, I overheard the stationmaster talking with a lanky middle-aged man dressed in Levi's and chaps. He wore a grey homespun shirt with faded red bandana. A sweat-stained Stetson topped off his outfit. He was trying to sell some recently tamed stock to the stagecoach company and seemed somewhat down on his luck.

I led Chino out of the stall and moved closer to the conversation. The stationmaster agreed to purchase his five horses at fifteen dollars a head. It wasn't much, but it was eating money for a while. I thought back to the times when I did the same thing. My pa always said, "When the chips are down, horseflesh is money, Son." I never forgot that.

After the preliminary haggling, the stationmaster went to draw up the Bill of Sale.

I turned to the man saying, "Hi there. I couldn't help but hear part of your conversation. Are you looking for a job?"

He turned to me and by the look on his face, he noticed the star on my shirtfront. "Hello, Marshal. Why, yes. I am in need of a job. A couple of friends and I have been looking for full time work for some time now. Do you know of a place hiring?"

I looked into the hopeful hazel eyes and asked him what his best work was and to my delight, he replied, "We are looking for horse-type work. The three of us are wranglers and horse hunters. What we don't know about horses ain't been discovered. By the way, Marshal, I am Judd Ellison."

I shook his hand. It was hard and callused, as though he had handled many a rope. This man loved horses. I bet that he knew a hell of a lot about hunting them down and training them. I reflected on that mighty hard. I remembered that some men would rather starve than work for a woman.

I looked him eye to eye and said it straight out, "Judd, there is a horse ranch about an hour ride out of Miller's Station. That spread needs some good men. I have to warn you though, the spread is owned and run by a woman, and right just now, she can't pay much."

"No kidding?" was his response.

"No kidding, Judd, but this lady is some kind of woman. She rides like a wild Comanche. She hunts down, breaks, and trains wild stuff, and you ought to see her ride. I watched her ride a young black and it was "who-flung-the-chunk?" all the way. She sat that horse like she was born there and in the end—well, let's just say that today, Mickey is her favorite mount."

I continued, "Miss Sumner is running alone right now, and needs all the help that she can get—especially from the likes of honest men like yourself. She hunts down horses in the wilds and then breaks them to saddle stock. She is trying hard to make a go of it by herself, and needs some hands that will stick it out come hell-or-high-water. As a matter of fact, if you were to show up with a couple of horse savvy men with you, you might be hired as foreman."

I pondered a bit to make my point before saying, "Were I some sort of wrangler myself, I would be a-hot-footing-it to her range right now. After all, there's bound to be some kind of drifters looking for a job and a meal or two."

Ellison looked at me with the spark of hope in his eyes, "You don't say. Yah, Marshal, I reckon that I might take a ride that direction. There sure ain't much work around here. Can I use your name, in case I do go to Miller's Station?"

"Certainly," I replied. "Tell Miss Laura Sumner that Cole Stockton sent you."

Ellison looked at me intently as he reflected a bit. "You're not *the* Cole Stockton, are you? I mean, Cole Stockton, the gunfighter?"

"Yes, Judd, I am that Cole Stockton. However, I am Marshal Stockton now."

Judd nodded his understanding, "No offense, but I heard some God-awful stories about you. There are some that say that only a devil could be as fast as you with them guns. There are a lot of men that I know, cowboys and wranglers and such, that wish they could be like you. Myself, I just want to work with horses."

He continued, "I ain't no gunfighter—never wanted to be one neither. I think a lot while I'm out on the range and I figure that a man like you can't afford to have many friends. You ain't like them other fellers I've seen that fancied themselves as fast guns. I would be justly proud to call you a friend."

"Thanks, Judd. Anyway, should you get a hankering for some of the best grub you ever ate, head on down to the Sumner ranch. Like I said, rustle up about a half dozen or so like riders that like good food and could weather a storm of short pay for a while, just until she gets her feet on the ground. I feel sure that Miss Sumner would talk with you."

The stationmaster came up just then with the Bill of Sale and some cash money in hand. I bid my farewell and led Chino around to the coach. Smith and Jacobs along with the town marshal and two deputies had our special passengers ready to board. Ex-banker Smith looked to have lost a pound or so. Jack Wakely glared at me with bloodshot eyes and his former deputy hung his head as they climbed groaning into the coach to sit in their assigned seats.

The driver and shotgun rider climbed to the box and with the snap of a whip shouted, "Hee Haw! Come on my pretties, lean into them harnesses!" The coach rocked forward amidst a few swearwords from the prisoners inside. I touched spur to Chino's flank and as we loped ahead, a silly grin spread across my face. Judd Ellison was sure to show up at Laura's ranch, and I felt good about it.

*   *   *

The next two days travel proved uneventful. Upon arrival in Denver, I had the driver pull up in front of the Territorial Jail. One by one, the sad-faced prisoners climbed out of the coach. Jailers stepped up and took charge of the men. I accompanied them into the office and wrote out the charges on each, glad to finally have them off my hands.

I rode Chino to his own stable where I unsaddled, rubbed him down with fresh straw and filled his feeder with hay and a handful of grain. I saw to fresh water in his bucket. Now, it was time to report my doings to Judge Wilkerson.

Word of my arrival had preceded me. Henry ushered me directly in to give my report to the judge. "Come in, come in, Marshal Stockton. I've been waiting for you. Who do we have in custody and what are the circumstances?"

I related my observations of Wakely and his thugs, the shootings at the Sumner ranch, and the information given by the dying raider before he passed. I told of my shoot out at the jail and of arresting the banker, Julius Smith, in possession of a satchel full of the townspeople's money. I further informed him of the demise of Jake Tanner and his boys.

The judge nodded his understanding of each detail before speaking, "Yes, Cole. A dying man's confession is worth a lot in court, and the fact that the banker identified Wakely as the shooter in the Jesse Sumner murder makes a good basis for trial. I suppose that each will hire a silver-tongued lawyer to try and outwit us; however, with a good solid testimony from the likes of my Deputy U. S. Marshal, Cole Stockton, I think that we can safely assure a speedy verdict on each case. You did a good job, Marshal Stockton—Cole."

With a slight twinkle in his eye, Judge Wilkerson mused, "I suppose that you found this Miss Sumner a very likeable young woman. Every time you mentioned her name, your face lit up."

And, then the judge leaned back in his chair and laughed out loud. Of course, I was dumbfounded. I had no idea that my feelings for Laura could be read so easily. He was still chuckling as he waved me off saying, "Take a day or two off to rest. I've got some more assignments for you."

CHAPTER FIFTEEN

Boss Wrangler

The day after Cole Stockton left Miller's Station with prisoners for Denver, Laura Sumner stepped out on her porch around sundown to watch a rider pull into the ranch yard. She recognized him immediately and it caused a bitter taste in her mouth.

The rider reined his buckskin to a halt within a few yards of her. His dirty clothes looked as though he had slept in them. His greasy brown hair fell to his shoulders. Even from a distance, Laura caught the whiff of unwashed body. This unkempt man turned her stomach.

The young man slouched in the saddle. His eyes were bloodshot as though he had been drinking for quite a while and was suffering a hangover. His speech was slurred. "Evening, Miss Sumner. I came to ask you for my job back. I done rode all over creation and no one would hire me."

Laura looked at him with disgust, "Turner, you were the first to quit me when the going got rough. I wouldn't hire you back if you were the last wrangler on the face of this earth. Get off my land and never come back!"

Turner sneered at her, "You—acting so proud! Someone ought to take you and whup you into a respectful woman. Come to think about it, I just might do it now." He started to dismount.

Laura placed her hand on the butt of her Colt Lightning, "Turner, you set one foot off that crowbait, I'll fill you so full of lead it will take a blacksmith to dig it out. I say this for the last time. Get off my land and stay off it!"

Turner looked down at Laura's hand on the revolver and relented, "O.K., I'll go. But, mark my words, I'll be back. You'll beg me to work for you. Why, there ain't no man within a hundred miles that will work for a woman. You got to have a *man* run this here place. I'll give you two days. I'll be back and then iffen you want wranglers, I will be the man to talk to. I done talked to every man looking for a job in this area. No one will work for you. You are going to go broke and the bank will foreclose on this spread. You will have come here for nothing."

Laura gritted her teeth for an instant. She was mad as hell. Her hand flashed suddenly and in the next instant, Lyle Turner was staring down the bore of her Colt.

"If you aren't off my land in ten seconds, I'll empty this gun straight into your lying, no good, intimidating hide. Mark my words, Turner. If you ever set foot on this range again, I'll shoot you where I find you."

Lyle Turner jerked his stringy horse hard around and with a mean scowl rode out the main gate of the Sumner ranch. Laura exhaled with a rush. Turner, however foul that he may be, was right. She couldn't possibly save this ranch without help. She was in dire need of good, experienced wranglers—men who would stay with her.

Laura stood there, her eyes closed in prayer. Momentarily the tears came, flooding her eyes. She holstered the revolver, then dashed into the house, flinging herself on her bed. She cried for a long time.

Laura knew that she had to have men who would work hard from daylight to dusk; she had to have men who would support her, men who would work for a woman. She shook her head, "Uncle Jesse, am I beaten? Are there any men who will work for me, a woman? I need your help Uncle Jesse. Please tell me what to do."

She was repeating her prayer as she slipped into a deep slumber. She dreamed of a well-stocked horse ranch with many stallions and many mares. She dreamed of selling a great many horses to people who paid handsome prices. She dreamed of making a go of the Sumner ranch, and of having respect from other ranchers in the area.

*　　*　　*

The following day, Laura rode the wilds searching for signs of wild horses. She rode all morning and by mid-day she hadn't crossed a single trail. "I've got to have help. I can't possibly cover all the ground that needs to be covered without help. Dear God, please send me some help."

Discouraged, Laura turned Mickey toward home. An hour later, she dismounted Mickey wearily, rubbed him down, then stabled him. She placed extra oats into his feeder. Then, the tired horsewoman walked forlornly toward the house.

Halfway to the house Laura saw four riders turn into the gates of the Sumner ranch. She took a deep breath, moving her right hand close to the butt of her revolver. "Oh, Lord, what now?"

The four men rode straight toward her, before stopping only yards from her. "Howdy, Ma'am," called out the front rider. "Would you be Miss Laura Sumner?"

Laura looked over the men cautiously before answering, "Why, yes I am. What business do you have here?"

The leader of the group swept off his dusty hat and holding it in front of him announced, "Miss Sumner, I hope we ain't no bother, but a man I met in Pueblo a few days ago told me that you might have need of a few good horse wranglers. Well, me and the boys talked it over and to tell the truth, we know about your money situation. We are willing to stick it out, providing that the grub is like that man said. He told me that there was no better cook, and no better food than right here. Miss Sumner, we boys would rather eat good than collect full pay until you can afford to sum up the wages. In other words, Miss Sumner, we want to work for you, that is, if you will have us. We aren't all exactly the best, but we will try."

Laura felt the tears of fulfilled prayer coming to her eyes, and she sniffed a bit. Immediately, all four men dismounted and turned their utmost attention to her. "Did we frighten you? Did we offend you? We don't mean no harm. If there ain't no job, just tell us. We will ride out and look further."

Laura searched each man's face and saw sincerity. She struggled to hold back tears of joy as she read each man's makeup. These were honest men. She swallowed the lump in her throat and announced, "No, you didn't offend me. I am just overwhelmed that so many men would come here at this very moment. Yes, I want to hire wranglers, but right now I can't pay much. As a matter of fact, I am almost broke. It will take a good-sized herd to sell in order to pay anything at all. I'm sorry, but that's all I can offer—my word that you will get paid for all your work."

The leader spoke again for the group, "Ma'am, we are just out of riding the starving line. We haven't found horse work in a long time, some of us in as much as six months. We've cut wood for a meal. We've chased down stray cows for a meal. We've even mended farm fences for a meal. We are each looking for a home. Like I said, a man I met at the stagecoach station in Pueblo told me of your plight. We talked it over, and we are willing to do whatever it takes to get the job."

The spokesman's words seared through Laura's mind like a bolt of lightning, "Just who was it that sent you here? What are your names?"

The men smiled warmly as the leader explained, "Miss Sumner, I am Judd Ellison and I come here with my friends. A man by the name of Cole Stockton told me of your plight. He also said that you put out a spread of vittles that a man could normally only dream about. Matter of fact, he put it this a way, 'Them freshly baked biscuits were sopping with freshly churned butter and dripping with pure honey.' That, Miss Sumner is heaven to a wrangler. We like to earn what money we get, but most of all, we love good food."

Laura's face softened as she looked at the four men in front of her, "Give me two hours and we'll have a good supper. In the meantime, stable your horses and take your things to the bunkhouse. You are all hired, that is, if you still want the job."

Judd's eyes lit up like a small child on Christmas morn. The other three men sighed with a rush of wind and replied, "Yes, Ma'am. We are your men now. We will do whatever you want. Just tell us what you need done and we will do it."

Laura turned to the house and upon entering began to cry. Tears of joy streamed down her face as she fired up the cast iron stove and began to prepare a meal for her new wranglers and herself. The vision of a good horse ranch was once more at the forefront of her mind. Silently, she once again thanked the man who had somehow intervened in her life. Was it fate?

Once more the words of Maude Pritchard came to Laura, "There will be one, a man born of deadly skill. There will be love; there will be honor. Through him you will have many adventures." Laura

Lynne Sumner thought of Cole Stockton and a warm smile spread slowly across her face. Her eyes turned soft and a tremble moved through her body.

*   *   *

Some two hours later four very hungry wranglers sat around Laura's porch with plates piled high. She marveled at their appetites. They ate like they hadn't had a square meal in over a month.

Tom Langdon finally put his plate down. Not a morsel remained as he rubbed his stomach saying, "Miss Laura, I don't know about these other three, but you have got yourself a wrangler from here on out. That was the best grub I ever ate." Judd and the other two sighed, nodding their heads in approval.

Laura grinned, "I hope that you boys aren't too full. There is a huckleberry pie warming in the oven."

A chorused reply was music to her ears, "Trot that pie on out here. We'll show you what some honest to goodness horse wranglers can do with a pie." Good-natured laughter followed. After pie and coffee, the men said their good-nights and heartfelt thanks before going to the bunkhouse for a good night's sleep. They promised to be ready for work shortly after sunrise the next day.

*   *   *

The next morning, the sun had just peaked over the eastern horizon when Laura stepped out to the porch of her house. She was suddenly grabbed from the left side and held firmly. The voice behind her was gruff with words slurred. Stale whiskey breath mingled with the stench of unwashed body.

Laura felt sick to her stomach as the perpetrator spoke, "I told you that I would come back here and teach you to mind yore manners. I'm going to whup you until you submit and hire me as the boss wrangler. Then, I will get some men to come and do this ranch's business."

Laura screamed as loud as she could. Suddenly, four men dashed out of the bunkhouse with rifles in hand and ran toward Laura.

Lyle Turner was taken unaware. He had no idea that there were four men on the grounds. He loosened his grip on Laura for just an instant. She squirmed hard to get out of his hold, then kneed him straight in the groin. Turner doubled over in pain as he fell to the porch. Immediately, four men stood over Turner with grim looks on their faces. Laura stepped a few paces back and pointed at the man, "Boys, this is Lyle Turner. I fired him because of his nasty attitude my first day here. I didn't want him on this ranch then, and I certainly don't want him here now."

Judd scowled at Turner with disgust, "Well, boys, we got us an intruder that would do harm to our boss. What shall we do to teach this hombre some manners and convince him that he ain't welcome on this range?"

Turner's eyes went wide as suggestions moved around the circle of men. "Hell, Judd, let's just hang him. After all, he accosted a lady, not to mention, our boss. We just don't take kindly to that kind of behavior around our home."

"Better yet, Judd, let's tie him to the training post in the center of the corral and hoss whip him a time or two."

And yet another thought out loud, "No, Judd, I've a far better idea. Let's tar and feather him, then ride him out the gates on a rail. We'll show him what we do to undesirables who sneak in here like a thief in the night and accost a lady."

Laura stood there listening to every word. Judd Ellison turned to her and with soft voice asked, "Well, boss, what do *you* want us to do with this scum?"

Her response was quick and to the point, "Judd, I just want him off of this ranch. I want him to understand that he is not wanted here ever."

Judd nodded his head, "It will be done, Miss Laura. Now, if you would please go back into the house for a few minutes, we will give this man a message that he will not long forget."

Laura feared for Turner's miserable life. She searched Judd's eyes and found the glint of mischief. He winked at her and in that moment she knew that no real harm would befall Turner. She turned and entered her house. Once inside, she crept to the curtains and carefully peered out to watch.

Turner trembled all over as he heard the words, "All right, intruder, shuck them duds, all the way down to your long handles." He cowered against the outside wall of the house, "What? What are you going to do to me?"

Again came the command, "You got a choice, take off them clothes or be whupped by four men until you can't see straight."

Turner slowly undressed to his filthy underwear. His buckskin horse was brought up to the porch and the four wranglers gleefully mounted Turner backwards in the saddle. Taking Turner's own lariat, they tied him there securely. His grimy clothes were stuffed into his saddlebags and his pistol emptied of all cartridges. His gun and belt were then draped over the saddle horn.

Judd made it plain and clear, "Turner, if you ever set even one foot on this range again, I will personally whup the living daylights out of you. After that, every man on this ranch will have his go with you. You may whip some of us, but I will guarantee that you will get the beating of your miserable life. You come back here with a gun; all of us will shoot you on sight. Now, I surely hope that your horse knows his way back to town, because if he don't, you will have to tell him where to go."

There was a muffled silence for only a moment and then four voices spoke as one, "Hee Yaw. Get up there, hoss!"

Laura watched as the buckskin jumped straight into a bouncing lope and Turner was jolted up and down, wincing all the way out of the gate. The horse turned toward town and within minutes there was only a dust cloud hanging loose in the air.

Laura smiled first, then broke into uncontrollable giggles. This was good old wrangler fun, mostly reserved for newcomers, and *tenderfoot E*asterners. It would be extremely embarrassing for Turner to be seen by all as his horse trotted through Main Street of Miller's Station, especially if it turned into the hitching post at a saloon. Turner would have a hard time living this down.

A soft knock came at the door. Laura stepped quickly to it and opened it to look into Judd's delightfully smiling hazel eyes. She smiled widely, "Thank you. Thank all of you. I wanted justice but, but," her voice trailed off.

"We understand, Miss Laura. We ain't hard men. We are just what we are—horse wranglers and nothing more. We couldn't do any real harm to a man, but we sure can make it plain to those that ain't wanted here."

Judd continued, "We ride for our boss and whatever the boss says is law. You'll find that us four are the best of friends, even at our worst. For the most part, we ain't had no book learning, but we know the rights and wrongs. You have entrusted us with a duty and to that end, we will support you. Never worry, Miss Laura, we will always be by your side. By the way, I drew up a short list of names. I put out the word before I left Pueblo, and should any of these men show up you will have one of the best group of horse handlers in the West."

Laura paused for a moment before addressing Judd, "Judd, I want *you* to be my foreman. Will you accept?"

Laura watched as Judd stood speechless. He hung his head for a moment. When he looked up he responded with, "Miss Laura, I accept. I will do you proud. I will take care of you and this ranch. Together, we will make this the best horse ranch in the Territory. You have my promise on that."

* * *

The very next morning Laura Sumner stepped out to her porch dressed in her horse-hunting outfit. She wore her "lucky" black Stetson. She looked up and smiled. Directly in front of her were four grinning wranglers mounted, with Mickey saddled and waiting for her.

It was Judd that asked, "Well, Boss Wrangler, where do we ride today?"

"Judd, I was thinking about the area close to the foothills of the Rockies. That is really rugged country and I am sure that there is more wild stuff hiding there than we can shake a stick at." Laura's boys nodded their heads affirmatively.

Laura swung up into Mickey's saddle and the group rode out the gates toward the distant foothills. She watched the men as they rode. Their eyes continually searched the horizon and the ground. They were honest to goodness horse hunters.

By noon they hadn't found a single trail. Laura remarked as such. Judd pondered only a moment before answering, "Miss Laura, you're the boss, but I think that we are in the wrong place. Look over there. See that low slope toward the rocky pass. If I were a wild horse, that's where I would go. We need to look for small creeks, and less traveled areas. Wild stock avoids the more traveled areas. Once we find their pattern and their trails we will have the way of them."

Laura looked at Judd. The man spoke good sense. Uncle Jesse's words came to mind. "Look for them horses in the most peculiar places—them places that ain't traveled. Find their watering holes and their grazing land. You do that, my dear niece, and you will find horses enough."

Laura nodded affirmatively so the group turned toward the west. Within an hour, there were so many fresh prints that you couldn't count the horses.

Judd turned in the saddle and addressed the group, "All right, boys, you know what to do."

The wranglers spread out, riding easy in the saddle. All at once, they turned in toward the trail and jumped their mounts straight into an easy trot. They kept the pace until some long minutes later. One of the largest wild horse herds that Laura had ever seen loomed into view.

Laura's heart thumped wildly. She watched as a magnificent black stallion reared to its hind legs, his front hooves pawing the air as he sounded the alarm. The herd broke into a hard gallop with the stallion holding back to urge them onward. Suddenly, the black broke directly into a ground-eating run to the forefront of the herd leading it to wilder country. He was the leader, and he was fast. He was the most beautiful stallion Laura had ever seen, with powerful muscles that rippled as he made his getaway. His mane and tail were like banners in the late afternoon sunlight. Laura nodded her head, whispering to herself, "One day—one day, you will be mine, you magnificent creature."

The wranglers broke first into a gallop, loosening their lariats as they rode purposefully toward the center of that herd. Next, they touched heel to their mounts and were into a dead run, lariats swinging.

Laura rode Mickey in amongst the herd, selecting a solidly build sorrel. The horse was fast. She gritted her teeth as Mickey followed every turn and evasive move that the horse made. She rose slightly in the saddle as she swung her rope, and then let it fly.

The loop sailed through the air and settled expertly around the sorrel's neck. She quickly tied off her end around the saddle horn. Mickey felt the pressure of the tie and slid to a halt. The rope reached end and the sorrel jerked back, to turn and shake its head. Without warning, it ran straight at Mickey with teeth bared, looking to bowl over the small black and rider.

The sorrel was only a few yards from Laura when another loop sailed around his neck, then slipped tight. The sorrel jerked quickly to the left and went to its knees for an instant, floundering, then rose to wobbly legs. It was shaken, but still solid horseflesh.

Laura thought that the horse was hurt, but as it stood shaking its head, she realized that it was only dazed. Laura looked over at Judd Ellison. "Sometimes, Miss Laura, one will come at you. That's why we normally work in pairs." Laura looked somewhat embarrassed. She had forgotten one of Uncle Jesse's foremost rules of horse hunting. "Always work in pairs when you can. Them horses will try every which way they know to get out of your clutches."

Judd grinned, "Don't take it too awful hard, Miss Laura. Even *we* forget sometimes, especially when watching a horse like that black that rushed to the front of the herd. Man, he is something else. That was a sight to behold. That is the animal to catch."

Laura looked back to the dust swirl that only moments before held well over two hundred head of wild horses. She watched as her boys returned from different quadrants of the herd. All the men had at least two beautiful mares in tow, and they were all grinning from ear to ear.

It was Chuck Wilson who spoke up, "Got the girls, Miss Laura. The boys will trail and come for them." They were half way back to the ranch when Laura looked behind her. There were at least twenty more horses following them. The bunch was made up of several colts, foals, and fillies. Another mare had joined the group also.

Judd rode beside Laura, and raised his finger to his lips to signal silence. Very slowly and without words, two of Laura's new wranglers handed the lead ropes of their captured mares to Judd and Tom Langdon, then quietly spread wide to opposite sides. The straggling horses moved closer in to the mares and then the out riding wranglers closed in along each side of them.

Laura looked questioningly at Judd. He grinned back at her, saying in soft tones, "Sometimes this works, sometimes it don't, but it was worth a try. Well, we got a few horses this afternoon. There will be more yet to come, count on it. Miss Laura, I can't help but to mention it. That Black in the lead—well, I think that we just got to study on that animal. That is the most beautiful piece of horseflesh that I have ever seen. You could build a real horse ranch with him as stud. We need to come back here tomorrow to follow them tracks. We need to plot out his stomping grounds and one day, you can bet your bottom dollar, you will have him on this ranch."

Laura listened to him intently before she replied, "Judd, did you see the way that he broke straight into that run? His mane was just flying and his tail held high as if to say, 'catch me if you can.' He was like the wind, those powerful muscles, rippling with every stride. Judd, I want that horse for our ranch. Help me catch him."

"Miss Laura, it is going to take time, a couple of weeks—even a month or two, but, yes, we will be the ones to catch him. I know what I am talking about. You see, we boys will memorize his prints. Every evening, we will talk, and plot on a map, the area in which he ranges. There will be a pattern. We will ride that pattern and narrow down his favorite places. One day, and I will promise you this, one day, we will be waiting for him."

"Yes, Judd, one day I will be waiting for him. I *want* that black stallion."

*   *   *

In the late afternoon, Laura and her four wranglers with horses in tow rode into the ranch yard. There were two men sitting on Laura's porch. Both of their horses appeared well trained by the way that they were ground hitched at the water trough.

Laura glanced over at Judd. He spoke up, "It looks like my word got out. We got us a couple of horse handlers to talk to."

The other wranglers turned the horses into the large corral area while Laura and Judd peeled off and rode directly to the house. Laura looked over the two men as she rode up to them and read their makeup. One man was young. He looked to be about nineteen. The other man appeared to be in his mid-forties, and he wore a gunbelt slung low. Both looked relaxed.

The two men rose and removed their hats as Laura and Judd dismounted. The older of the two addressed Judd, "Howdy, Judd. I got wind that you were looking for wranglers and decided to check in."

The younger of the two introduced himself, "Hi, I am Mike Wilkes. I don't have much experience, but I love horses. I have ridden for a couple of farms east of here and I want to learn to be a real horse hunter."

Judd looked over at Laura. She swallowed a bit hard, nodding to him. Judd looked hard at the older man. "Eli Johnson. You are right in a way. I put the word out for wranglers. You are a good one, I admit that, but you have always carried that hogleg like a part of you, and there has been some trouble over it. You fancy yourself as a gunman. I am sorry, Eli. There is no place for a would-be gunman on this ranch."

Eli nodded, "I see. All right, Judd. I respect you. Thank you for telling me right out. I'll be leaving directly."

Laura stepped back and pulled Judd to her side. She stared at the ground. Finally, she spoke under her breath, "Judd, we might need someone with shooting ability. If you know this man and he can be trusted, explain my situation and speak to him about the gun. It is your decision, however, right now, I can't turn away good men."

Judd softly replied, "All right, Miss Laura. I can vouch for him as a very good horseman. I will speak to him about the gun."

Laura cocked her head for a moment as she studied Mike Wilkes. She turned to Judd with a pleasant smile, and with a slightly musical tone of voice, said, "Hire the young man also. I like his makeup. Teach him, Judd. Make him a good wrangler."

"Yes, Ma'am," replied Judd, turning again to Wilkes, "Wilkes, you are hired. Stable your mount and move your gear into the bunkhouse. Eli, hold on there a minute, I need to talk with you."

Mike Wilkes gratefully took his bay by the reins and led it toward the stables.

Judd stepped up to Eli Johnson. "Eli, the Boss Wrangler says that I should talk further with you. Let me put it straight. I'm going to save your miserable hide, maybe. I came to this job through a man that I met at the stagecoach station in Pueblo. I think I know Miss Laura, and the way that I have it figured is that my friend and Miss Laura are v-e-r-y good friends. Can you grasp the gist of that? Now, I know you pretty well. You have always figured yourself to be somewhat of a gunman. Well, I'll tell it to you straight. Miss Laura's friend is none other than Cole Stockton."

Judd watched Eli's eyes flash for a moment, "Judd, you mean *the* Cole Stockton? I mean, the one who them stories are about?"

"Yah, Eli, and I am here to tell you that if I hire you, the condition is that you take off that gunbelt and never carry anything but a Winchester rifle while you are working with us. I have a strong feeling that Mr. Stockton will be back and that there will be enough lead flying without having to worry about you. O.K., Eli, accept them terms or be on your way. I will not have a would-be gunman working on this ranch. There are too many other good men looking for a job."

Eli studied Judd for a moment. "Judd, you are right. I always did favor to be famous with the gun. I surely wish that I could have been, but Cole Stockton—Man-Oh-Man, Lordy, I tremble just thinking about even seeing him in the flesh. I've heard that men who have faced him took one look into his eyes and saw the Angel of Death. It's said that he carries the fire of hell itself in his eyes. God, Judd, can you even imagine that?"

"Yah, Eli, I can. I've met the man. Anyways, you want the job, give me your gunbelt and don't never touch nothing but a Winchester while you work here. I catch you with any kind of revolver, you are gone—fired."

"All right, Judd. Here's my gun." Ellison took the belt and revolver. The foreman nodded his head, then motioned toward the bunkhouse, "Eli, go and stow your gear. Supper should be ready in a couple of hours. Eli! Don't ever go back on your word with me, because I would feel awful bad to have to bury you."

"Shucks, don't worry none about me, Judd. I am a man of my word."

"I know, Eli. I know." Jud looked at the gunbelt in his hand. The Colt was well cared for. He slipped the revolver out of the holster and flipping open the loading gate, began to eject cartridges from the cylinder. He counted six, and shook his head, "Even Stockton only carries five. His hammer sits on an empty chamber for safety reasons. He only loads the sixth one if he feels that he needs it, and that ain't very often."

Judd walked up the steps of the house and lightly rapped on the door. It was opened within moments by Laura. "Miss Laura, I hired both of them. I made Eli promise to never carry anything but a rifle while working on this ranch. He goes back on that, I fire him."

"That's fair enough, Judd. You are my foreman and what you say goes."

"Thank you for your confidence, Miss Laura. We will do this ranch mighty proud. I think that there will be more honest to goodness wranglers coming soon. This is only the first couple of men. Before long, we can choose just who we want, and I know a few that we need to hire in order to get this here ranch back on its feet. Should I not be here for some reason, and an older man, name of Scotty, shows up, hire him on the spot. He will probably want something like fifty dollars a month. Let him taste your vittles, then offer him thirty dollars and meals. That man loves to eat."

CHAPTER SIXTEEN

Laura In Peril

The next morning, Laura dressed in her trail clothes, prepared breakfast for the wranglers, then joined the men at the stables. Judd Ellison commented, "No need to come with us today, Miss Laura. After all, that's why you hired us. We are going to track and plot today. If we find some horses, we will bring them back. Think about my plan; however, you do as you like."

Laura paused for a moment, then lifted her eyes to the group, "I'm sorry, boys. It has just been so long since I've had any help that—well, it's just that I'm not used to having men with good judgment work for me."

Judd turned to the others with a grin, "Hear that, fellers? Our Boss Wrangler ain't never had no help like us. Let's go find Miss Laura some good horses." With that, they turned as one and rode out toward the distant foothills at the base of the Colorado Rockies.

Laura watched them go and felt proud. She returned to the house thinking, "Those boys will be hungry when they come back. I am going to cook up a large beef cottage pie. There must be biscuits a plenty, and lots of coffee. My boys deserve the best that I can do."

* * *

While Laura busied herself in the kitchen, a burly gunman surveyed the Sumner ranch yard as he slowly rode his dun to the house. He saw no one about the area. An evil grin adorned his face as he guided his mount to the left side of the porch and dismounted. The woman, he was told, was attractive and that thought stirred his blood. Quietly, he walked up the steps to the door.

Laura was so involved with her kitchen work that she didn't notice the rider enter the ranch yard. She was suddenly startled by

119

the hard knocking at the front door. She set the large pan of potatoes to the side of the stove and stepped through the front room.

As a quick thought, Laura reached to the peg holding her gunbelt and withdrew the Colt Lightning revolver, tucking it behind her belt. She stepped to the door and opened it.

Laura peered directly into the dark eyes of death. She inhaled sharply, involuntarily stepping backward. The evil man lunged toward her, "I was sent by a man that wants you dead and has paid me my price. I intend to take my pleasure before I kill you."

Laura fumbled for the revolver as the man grabbed both of her arms tightly. She winced in pain, still trying desperately to reach the Colt tucked behind her belt. The man was too strong, he pushed himself down on her and they crashed to the floor in a writhing struggle.

Laura inhaled the foul odor of hard whiskey breath as he wrestled for control. Suddenly, he ripped her shirt open, exposing her camisole covered breasts. His eyes were wild with lust and his lips curled in cruelty. Saliva oozed from the corners of his mouth. He held her even tighter than before as he fumbled with her belt to rip open her Levi's. Laura screamed while she tried to fight him off, but he was too strong. He overpowered her and she felt hopeless. She prayed for a quick death.

Suddenly a sharp male voice broke through the scuffle. It came from behind them, along with an unmistakable click of metal as the newcomer cocked his revolver. The strong voice was deadly as he commanded, "Unhand that woman, and prepare to meet your maker, Dixon!"

Jules Dixon, caught in the act of raping Laura, turned quickly to stare at the man behind them. His eyes went wide with surprise, as he stuttered out the name, "Carlson!"

"Damn right, Dixon. Your murdering days are over. You are a dead man."

Dixon rolled away from Laura Sumner, pawing for his gun. His hand closed around the butt of the weapon and he turned to face the newcomer when the sharp crack of thunder reverberated through the house. Dixon slammed backward with the hammer of death burning deep in his chest.

Matt Carlson stepped forward and shot Dixon once again, straight between the eyes. Within the ensuing silence, Carlson slowly holstered his weapon. A moment later, he turned to help Laura to her feet. He looked away briefly as she adjusted her clothing.

"Ma'am, I'm downright sorry about these circumstances, that you had to suffer this. Jules Dixon was a most vicious killer. I tracked him for five months and now I finally caught up to him. This man raped and killed Rebecca, my fourteen-year-old daughter, over in Arkansas five months ago. I been tracking him ever since. I will drag this trash out and bury him. Finally, I can go home."

He paused for a moment before continuing, "By the way, don't worry none about Lyle Turner anymore. He's the one that hired this scum. That's how I knew where Dixon was headed. I accosted Turner with some pointed questions and he went for his gun in the most miserable draw that I ever seen. I shot him dead an hour ago."

Laura regained her composure and rearranged her clothing a bit more. Shakily, she swallowed with hoarseness, then asked, "Would you stay a while, Mr. Carlson? My wranglers should be back within the hour. I would be honored if you would stay and have supper with us."

Carlson answered, "Ma'am, I sure would like to stick around, but to tell the truth, I am feeling sickly in the pit of my stomach right now. I'd never killed a man till I started this hunt. Forgive me, I just need to retch my stomach right now." Carlson turned abruptly and dashed out the door.

Laura heard the retching sounds as she reached behind her back to touch the butt of her Colt revolver. She knew that she had to be infinitely more careful from now on. Uncle Jesse's words filtered through her mind, "That country needs a good man with a gun. I ain't seen the likes of one yet that can strike fear into the hearts of those that would do harm to a body, but it would take a hard man—one born to the gun. And then, there might be law and order."

Laura's mind flashed to a name. A shiver brought the vision of the tall lanky man known as Cole Stockton. She remembered his easy manner and shy grin. Most of all she recalled his eyes when he looked at her. She saw strong admiration, respect, and his honor. Maude Pritchard's voice seemed to whisper in her ear as Goosebumps prickled her body, "One will stir the fires of your very soul. He is born of deadly skill, but through him, you will have many adventures. There will be love."

Laura stepped out to the porch steps and gently placed her hand upon Carlson's shoulder. He turned to face her. With solemn words, she told the man who had saved her life that she understood his pain. "Please stay. It's the least that I can do."

"Of course," he replied, "I'll stay for supper. Perhaps you might have an extra bed in your bunkhouse. I'll stay until tomorrow, and then I must begin the journey home to my wife in Arkansas. She must be terribly worried about me. I haven't written in months."

An hour or so later, Judd Ellison, Mike Wilkes, Eli Johnson, and the three other wranglers rode into the ranch yard with another twenty range stock. Judd rode up to the house while the others turned the stock into the holding corral. He dismounted at the hitching rail, stepped up to the porch and rapped on the door.

Laura opened the door, "Judd, I'm glad that you boys are back. I want you to meet someone." Laura took Judd into the kitchen and introduced him to Matt Carlson. She briefly told Judd the story.

Judd approached Carlson holding out his hand. "Thank you, Mr. Carlson. You are always welcome here on this ranch. Should you ever need a favor, or any help of some kind, let us know and you will have all the help you can ever want."

*   *   *

Matt Carlson rode back to Arkansas the next morning after a night's rest and hearty breakfast with Laura and her boys. He had been an honored guest and praised by all of Laura's men.

Judd pondered a decision, "Miss Laura, I think that we should have at least one man stay with you while the rest of us are riding the hunt."

Laura thought hard before replying, "No, Judd. We need to cover as much ground as we can. The time is growing close to pay our debts. We need all the horses that we can find and it will take all of us to do that. I will be alright by myself. I have learned a hard lesson. I promise to be very careful from here on out." Judd reluctantly agreed.

Three days later, Laura was once again alone and engrossed in slow cooking up a mess of beef ribs with a spicy sauce. "I'll just bet the boys will love this dish."

The windows were open to allow a cool breeze into the kitchen. From out of nowhere, she heard a horse whinny. She stopped and listened, then moved quickly through the living room, and peered out the curtains to see a stocky man she didn't recognize. He rode a large, powerful steel-gray horse and entered the yard riding slowly, taking in every inch of the ranch yard.

He eased back on the reins and his horse stopped dead still. The man raised his face a bit, and appeared to sniff the air. He smiled widely as he slowly moved his face from side to side. The man took one last very deep breath and then rode straight to the hitching rack where he dismounted. Standing at the bottom step of the porch, he hallowed the house.

Laura looked this man up and down. She felt no fear of this smiling newcomer; however, she reached to the rack beside the door and belted on her Colt Lightning revolver, settling it into place. She opened the door and stepped out onto the porch.

"Ah, Lassie, would that heavenly aroma happen to be spicy beef ribs in a thick tomato sauce? Would there be lot of mashed potatoes to go with it? Perhaps there are some nice flaky biscuits with freshly churned butter?"

"It might," said Laura, "and who might *you* be?"

"Ah, Lassie, I am but a poor roving Scotsman in search of a fine supper such as my taste buds have already alerted me. Pardon the intrusion, Missy, but a message came to me several weeks ago and I have been traveling here with most haste. An acquaintance of mine is seeking out the best horse wranglers on the frontier and I, Dear Lady, am only the best. I am called simply Scotty, no last names please. It would serve the King of Scotland only to find me and do me poor body harm. Tell me, would this be the Sumner ranch and is that fine fellow Judd Ellison about? Tell him that Scotty is here and my pay is fifty hard earned dollars a month."

Laura smiled knowingly. "Well, Mr. Scotty, I am Laura Sumner and this is my ranch. Judd Ellison is my foreman and should be back within the hour. Now, he said that you were a fairly good wrangler and that I should hire you at twenty dollars a month until you got more experience."

Scotty feigned a surprised scowl, "Why that highwayman! A fair wrangler says he? Does he think that I, Scotty, would work for novice wages? I think not. I will accept forty-five dollars a month and perhaps an occasional meal such as my nose now tells me is just about ready to eat."

"Mr. Scotty, if you are as good as you say that you are, I might go twenty-five dollars a month, and maybe, just maybe, throw in some Sunday meals."

"Dear Lass, I can see that we are merely haggling over my welfare. All right, I will work for forty a month and meals on Saturday and Sunday, but first, I must sample the wares of your cookery."

Laura took on a somewhat stern tone, "All right, wait right here and I'll get a sample of my beef ribs." She stepped to the side, then backed into the house. She got a plate from the cupboard and placed two large simmering ribs on it. As a second thought, she placed two large biscuits with butter on the plate as well. Laura returned to the porch, watching the man's eyes as he savored the ribs and biscuits. He held a rib to within two inches of his nose and deeply inhaled, "U-m-m-m, they smell delicious." He then tasted one and within only a minute or two had devoured every bit of meat on the bone and was delighting himself with the first biscuit. His eyes delivered admiration for Laura's culinary abilities.

Laura stated, "All right, Mr. Scotty, no more haggling. My final offer for the services of a most experienced horse wrangler is thirty a month, and meals every day."

Scotty's eyes shined brightly, "Good Lass, you have just outbid me. You have enriched my soul with your cookery. I shall be glad to render my services to you. I begin right after supper."

It was at that moment that Judd Ellison and the boys returned with yet another fifteen horses from the wilds. Judd rode over to the house and, looking at the empty plate in Scotty's hand, grinned widely. "Hello, Scotty. Glad you could make it. I presume that the Boss Wrangler has already hired you."

"Aye, Laddie. What a meal she has prepared this eve! Hurry now, Judd, get the wee beasties into the corral, for Miss Laura has said that I can't have any more of these fine beef ribs until all of our boys are ready to eat." Laura, Judd, and Scotty shared a good-natured round of laughter.

CHAPTER SEVENTEEN

A Reason To Celebrate

Early fall came to the Colorado Territory and several months had passed since Judd Ellison and the first of Laura's wranglers rode into the Sumner ranch yard looking for a job. It was hard work and Laura showed her mettle by riding frequently with her boys. They saw how well she rode, roped, and even stayed on the *wild whirlwind* until the horse was broken to saddle.

Laura accepted her share of the knuckle-busting, teeth-jolting, bone-jarring task of riding the wild ones into tameness, and the boys grew to respect her even more. Finally, over three hundred saddle broke horses were sold to the Army and a few to some miners. Laura had money enough to pay the debts due on the ranch as well as provide two months pay to each wrangler.

This particular Saturday morning meant a dance at the town meeting hall that evening. All of the wranglers were to work until noon, before they took their turns in the bath. Following baths, each would dress up in his Sunday-go-to-meeting best in order to turn the heads of local lasses. Each man was ready for an evening of socializing and entertainment.

Laura thought about the dance, but there was just no one to accompany her. About noon, Judd Ellison stepped upon the porch and rapped at the door. Laura opened the door to greet him, "Hi, Judd. I suppose the boys are anxious to attend the dance this evening. I certainly hope that they have a good time. They've earned it."

Judd grinned at her, "Miss Laura, the boys and I would sure like to escort you there. I know that we ain't the best of what you might call dancers, but we will try not to step on your feet too much. You also have earned a 'night to howl' as we would say."

Laura smiled at their kindness. Refusing to feel sorry for herself, she replied, "Thank you Judd. I would love to have all of you escort me to that dance. I can think of no other men that I would like to share this evening with."

Judd shuffled his feet a bit. He looked to be calculating something. Nodding his head, he mentioned, "I can, Miss Laura. I see it in your eyes every time you even think the man's name. To tell the truth, I saw it in his eyes, too, just a few months ago when I first met him. A man like that has got to have something to keep him going on them lonely trails. I kind've figure that it is you. Yes, Miss Laura, I believe that Cole Stockton keeps you in his mind when he is riding those lonely trails. I would dearly love to see the expression on both of your faces the next time that you meet. I would venture to say that if there was two people that were meant to be—well, I guess that you know what I am saying."

Laura couldn't speak. Judd saw the surprise, followed by the mist well up in her eyes.

"Yah, you do know what I am thinking. Sorry if I have upset you. Well, I figure that we'll ride into town around six this evening. There should be some good food at that shindig, so we'll stave off supper until we get there."

Laura smiled, "I'll be ready Judd, and, Judd—thank you."

*   *   *

Judd had several hands bring buckets of water to a fire they built out from the house and heated it up. Then, they carried the buckets of hot water into the house and filled Laura's galvanized bathtub up to a good measure. Laura languished in a full bath. Refreshed, she dressed in a deep blue gown for the dance. She also wore a simple ivory broach pinned above her right breast. It was one that her mother had given her. When she was ready, Laura stepped out on to the porch. All eyes were on her. The wranglers' eyes lit up with pride and appreciation for their boss lady.

"Come, Miss Laura, let me help you to the wagon." suggested Scotty. After she was comfortably situated on the wagon seat, Scotty drove the wagon to town, followed by all of the wranglers on horseback. Once in town, they took Laura straight to the meeting hall. Judd Ellison and Eli Johnson joined her on the boardwalk while the Scotty and the other wranglers went to park the wagon and stable their horses at the livery.

Laura, Judd, and Eli entered the large hall and glanced around at the colorful decorations. The many people in attendance milled around, speaking to those they knew. Ladies discussed the latest fashions in catalogs at the general store, and the men discussed the politics of the day as well as other *masculine* subjects. Eli ambled over to the liquid refreshment and food tables. Judd escorted Laura to a chair along the wall, then followed Eli Johnson for her punch.

Laura sat alone, observing other women who were busy chatting with friends. She thought that perhaps she should not have come. All of a sudden, she felt a shiver run straight up her spine that tingled through every inch of her body. Goose bumps spread along her arms. She looked around the hall, her eyes searching for a reason. She found him watching her from across the room. A warm smile broke across her face and her heart beat wildly as Cole Stockton strode across the dance floor to stand in front of her. He was dressed in a starched white shirt, string tie, and dark coat. The slight bulge of a revolver rested at his waist and she knew what it was.

Long moments passed as he stood motionless in front of her. They looked deeply into each other's eyes. Music began to play and he held out his hand to her. Mesmerized, she stood, then moved with him to the center of the dance floor. "I'm not too good at this dancing thing. I'll try not to step on your feet too much," Cole whispered.

Laura moved into his arms. Close together, they glided across the plank floor. Warmth flowed between them as they read the message in each other's eyes. If he stepped on her feet, Laura took no notice.

Judd Ellison stood along the wall holding two glasses of punch and watching. He grinned widely. Eli Johnson stepped up to him and remarked, "Now that is a great looking couple. Who is the gent dancing with Miss Laura? She looks taken with him."

Eli took a good sip of punch. Judd grinned from ear to ear with mischief, "Why, Eli, that there is Cole Stockton and our Boss Wrangler dancing together."

Eli choked on his punch, and Judd had to slap him on his back a couple of times to bring him around. It took Eli a moment to regain his composure and he swallowed hard, "Lord Almighty. I never thought that I would be in his company. Do you think that Miss Laura might just introduce us?"

"Maybe so, Eli, Maybe so," came the reply.

Just then, the song was over and both Laura and Cole Stockton walked to the men. Eli Johnson stood beside Judd with knees knocking together.

"Howdy, Judd, I see that you followed my advice and came up here. She's quite a woman, isn't she?"

"She sure is, Cole, and you were right about them vittles. Now, I have a friend here that has been just itching to meet you. He's a good wrangler, not too bright some times, but a good wrangler. Eli, meet Cole Stockton."

Eli Johnson stood awe-struck as he shook hands with Cole Stockton. He was face to face with the well known gunfighter turned lawman. Even though his palms were sweaty and beads of perspiration lined his forehead, the wrangler felt the Marshal's calm demeanor and captivating persona. Cole's eyes met Eli's as was his custom, and Eli felt the penetrating power of those eyes searching out his soul. An intense respect ran through his body as he said, "I am pleased to meet you, Mr. Stockton."

Cole smiled pleasantly as he replied, "It's good to meet you too, Eli. You are working with some good people. That says a lot about you."

Further conversation was interrupted by a commotion just outside the door to the meeting hall. A woman screamed.

Cole Stockton immediately turned and moved quickly to the entrance. Judd grabbed Eli by the shoulder, "Come on. Let's see what's going on." They forced their way through the crowd with Laura right on their heels.

Two men wearing guns were involved in a heated argument. A young woman stood to the side of them pleading, "Stop this nonsense and come back inside the dance."

One of the men continually waved her back with his hand as he addressed his opponent, "I'll teach you to put your hands on my girl, Boyd. Go on, reach for that hogleg."

The second man retorted, "She ain't your girl, Burke. She's my girl. Go ahead and ask her. She'll tell you the truth."

Without hesitation, Cole Stockton interrupted the men with a command, "Both of you men reach down with your left hand, unbuckle your gunbelts and let them drop. There will be no gunplay here tonight—unless I do it."

Les Burke turned his head to look at Stockton. "This here is a private matter, Mister, whoever you are. You're butting in where it don't belong. Let us be. We'll settle this between us."

"You'll end it now!" came the stern reply. "I'll shoot the first man that even touches his gun."

Burke turned to face Cole Stockton, "Well, maybe, I'll just take care of you first; then I'll tend to this miserable excuse for a man." Burke's hand slipped to his pistol butt and before he could clear the holster, there was the slick click of metal sliding against metal and he suddenly stared down the deadly bore of Stockton's Colt. The hammer was cocked back and ready. Burke's mouth dropped open as he stared into Stockton's eyes. He quietly let his revolver drop into the dirt street, trembling slightly as he stood there, with eyes wide and mouth open. It was as if he had looked into the immediate future and saw his own death.

"Like I said," Stockton repeated his command, "drop them gunbelts. You're both under arrest for disturbing the peace." Both men complied with the order, unbuckling and dropping their pistol belts into the street. Town deputies moved forward to collect the men and their guns. The rowdies were marched off to the jailhouse for the night.

Cole returned to Laura with a smile on his face. "Pardon the interruption, shall we go inside?" Arm in arm they stepped back into the evening's dance hall. The crowd in the street dispersed, most moving back to the dance. The music commenced and once again people danced and had a good time.

Eli Johnson stood just outside the meeting hall with Judd Ellison. He turned to look at Judd, shaking his head from side to side, "Judd—I never even saw the man's hand move and there it was, his Colt, cocked and ready. Judd, you can keep my revolver. I got no more use for it. I thought that I was a fair hand with that Colt, but I just seen something that changed my mind. And, them eyes, I looked into them eyes and I felt a searing on the edges of my very soul. Them stories are true, Judd, that man carries the gates of hell in his eyes."

At midnight when the band played their final piece, Laura stepped out on the boardwalk with Cole. They stood in the shadows for several minutes speaking quietly to one another. Laura's wranglers stood easy at their horses rolling themselves a smoke and talking quietly amongst themselves. They understood completely, their Boss Wrangler had a special friend and they were saying good night, for the next morning he would be escorting prisoners to the Territorial court in Denver.

Cole helped Laura to her seat in the wagon a short time later. He stepped back a bit and with a pleasant grin bid her farewell, until the next time. Laura smiled back at him, then turned to Scotty, "Alright, Scotty, take me home."

With her wranglers following, Laura rode the trail back to her ranch. Scotty looked at her and grinned. "Just what the devil has gotten into you, Scotty?" she asked.

"Oh, nothing, Missy. Nothing at all, except that I've seen that very same look on many a young lass in my old country. You, Miss Laura, are in love. That man needs to come back."

Laura reflected on Scotty's statement only a moment before replying, "Don't worry, Scotty. He'll be back. I made sure of that."

Scotty slapped reins to the wagon team and in jovial tone of voice, "Well, then, Boss Wrangler, let's go home."

CHAPTER EIGHTEEN

To Pay The Fiddler

Winter came and went. Spring was in the air along the Lower Colorado valleys. Although snow still capped the high peaks, the new grasses of the season were tender. Fish jumped in the rivers and streams.

I had been cooped up in the Denver office long enough. Since things were pretty quiet around the city, Chino and I decided to take a ride out to the closest stream and cool our heels so to speak. Chino grazed lazily along the embankment as I lay back on a flat rock—my boots and socks off and my feet idly dangling in the coolness of the creek.

Facing skyward, I watched puffy white clouds form objects to test the imagination. It's times like these that I get to thinking about my life. Here I am, an almost thirty year old man who rides the trails of misery and danger. It is, I suppose, the wildness in me, rather—the feeling there is usually something with more adventure over the next rise that keeps me from settling down.

Mostly though, it is that I seemed to be a natural born *kin to the gun*, and I proved it too many times. I want no woman and family to live with the fear that one day I won't come home because of a faster draw, or straighter shot. A man in my business gathers very few friends, and those that hold true are kept close to heart—yes, Laura Sumner is close to my heart.

We'd become quite close, and I'd visited her a few times over the past five or six months. It is daunting that during lonely nights on the trail of desperados, especially in the wilds of the territory, I vividly recall those crystal blue eyes reading my thoughts and speaking a silent language that only she and I understand.

I reflected, "How could anything else become of a relationship like that. Me, an older guy, and Laura, young, beautiful, and perceptive. A woman like that needs a like man to be with her."

I guess that you could say that in gun age, I was a very old man, having survived numerous vicious gunfights. You could also say that not many men of my profession live a long, full life. Wearing the star of authority with a marked reputation has its drawbacks, and the prospect of a special relationship didn't seem in the stars for me. Yet, time and time again, I was drawn to Laura, and I wondered, "Am I destined to be part of her life?"

*   *   *

Further south, near the town of Miller's Station, Laura Sumner finished dressing with a glance in the mirror before reaching for her gunbelt. Suddenly, the door to her room crashed open. Two rough grisly-bearded men burst into her room. Startled, she screamed, then turned toward her holstered pistol. It was too late. The taller of the two men held it in his hand.

They grabbed her roughly, tying her hands in front of her, then led her outside to the porch. Five riders held her hired hands at bay. "We're taking the horsewoman with us as insurance. You boys get that Marshal friend of hers here and she won't be harmed. He don't show, we don't promise nothing. You got just five days to have that Marshal Stockton in this area or else."

Another kidnapper yelled, "Yah, we want to talk to him about some friends of ours that he shot up. You can tell him that Sid Benton and Wylie Thompson have his lady friend and that he should come-a-running."

Presently, Mike Wilkes brought a saddled Mickey to the porch as the outlaws had ordered. They lifted Laura to her saddle, took her reins, turned, and led her out the gates of the Sumner ranch at a wild lope, laughing cynically.

Judd Ellison, Laura's foreman, turned to the others, "We've got to get her back, boys, let's saddle up."

Mike Wilkes looked at Judd Ellison with a forlorn face and said, "We're no gunmen, Judd. Besides, they said to get Marshal Stockton. Let's wire him directly. He'll know what to do."

Judd reflected only a moment before replying, "O.K., you're right. They said that Miss Laura would not be harmed—for the time being. They want to kill Marshal Stockton, you all know that!"

He continued, "Eli, get mounted and follow their trail. Hang back some so as not to be noticed. We at least can find out where they are taking her. I am riding to town to wire the Marshal's office. You boys keep the ranch running."

Judd reflected, "Them guys just don't know what they've got themselves into. There will be *hell to pay the fiddler* when Cole Stockton arrives."

*   *   *

My momentary solitude was abruptly interrupted by hoof beats, a cloud of dust, and the wild yelling of Jimmy Bowen, the young telegraph runner.

"Marshal Stockton! Marshal Stockton!" he yelled. "Where are you? Here! I've got an important telegram for you!"

Thinking that it was a damn good thing I wasn't fishing because I'd really be upset, I yelled out in reply while tugging my socks and boots on, "Over here, Son. What is this about a wire?" I rose and stomped my boots in place as Jimmy rode over to me, his hand extended with the wire.

"Comes from down at Miller's Station," he rattled on, "something about a horsewoman being kidnapped at gunpoint. They need you right away."

"That kid must read every telegram he carries," I mused. I took the crumpled wire from the lad and read it quickly. After a moment I solemnly replied, "Wire them back to say that I am on the way and will be there in a few days."

"Yessir, Marshal Stockton, I'll do that," replied Jimmy as he turned the dun and heeled it into a gallop back to town.

Turning to my roan, I stroked his muzzle whispering, "Come on, Chino, your lazy stable days are over for a while. We've got to help a friend." I knew, without a doubt, that those boys only wanted me, maybe. "Well," I contemplated, "let's not keep them waiting." I was never one to pussyfoot around when it came to facing the obvious.

Back at Ma Sterling's boarding house, it took only a few minutes to gather up my traveling gear along with some extra ammunition, and then I was off into the wilds of the Lower Colorado once again.

Late on my second day of travel when topping a rise, I caught the sounds of gunfire in the distance. Not one to avoid trouble, and quite willing to lend a helping hand when needed, I rode forward with haste to find some feller crouched behind his downed horse. He was firing at what appeared to be about a dozen renegade southern Cheyenne warriors.

They were attempting to ring him; I'll give him that he was good. The man kept up a steady fire to the sides of the group, pinning them down, as well as throwing hot lead into the center of the group. "This guy deserves saving," I muttered while drawing my Winchester. I levered a round into the chamber and began dusting the rear of the raider band. They sure as hell didn't like it. They gathered up their ponies and rode off to make trouble for someone else.

I rode cautiously up to the fallen horse and lo and behold! There lay my younger brother. Clay is tall and lanky, just like me, and he carries two Colt revolvers strapped around his waist. I'd never been with him during a real shoot out, but I heard tell through the grapevine that he was *hell on wheels* when it came to trading lead. The display of firearms that I just witnessed lent truth to that story. I guessed then that it must run in the family.

About that time, Clay struggled to his feet and with a good-natured snicker said to me, "About time you got here! I thought that I'd have to whup them all by myself."

I dismounted Chino, grabbed my canteen and handed it to him. "Not that stuff," he bellered. "Where's the good stuff?" Well, he figured me right. I retrieved my canteen and reached into my saddlebags to withdraw a small flask of whiskey that I carry for cold nights and medicinal purposes.

"Just what the hell are you doing out here in the Colorado Territory?" I questioned, having previously heard that he was a Territorial Marshal over in the Dakotas.

"I've been trailing the remnants of a gang that I partially shot up and jailed a few months back. It seems they swore revenge on me.

I just thought that I would give them the chance before they caught me when I wasn't looking."

That philosophy sounded vaguely familiar. I quickly explained about the taking of Laura Sumner.

Clay turned to me as he remarked, "Sounds like this is the same gang. Suppose they got us mixed up? These guys must have read something about a Marshal Stockton and the rustler problem in Colorado. Then, they figured that you was me. Well, Cole, I guess both of us could use a little help. You to get your friend back—me, to get the remainder of the gang."

It sounded like a good deal to me, so we both climbed up on Chino and slowly made our way to the Lower Colorado Valley. I recalled some fairly large ranches along our path of travel and as luck would have it, we were able to negotiate another mount for Clay.

Riding along beside my brother, I mused, "Oh boy, are those guys in for a surprise. They don't know it yet, but there are two Marshal Stocktons coming for them, and either one can be a handful when the chips are down."

Brother Clay and I arrived at the Sumner ranch at mid-morning on the third day. Judd Ellison and Eli Johnson came to us immediately. The other ranch hands followed close behind. I introduced Clay and then inquired of the critical information, "Tell me all you know about this kidnapping and where they might have headed." Judd prompted Eli, "Tell them about trailing the gang, Eli."

Eli Johnson recollected, "I followed them, hanging back some. They were crafty. They left two men lagging to scout their back trail for followers. I couldn't take the chance of being discovered, so I come back here and drew up a map of sorts." He rummaged into his shirt pocket, produced a folded paper, and handed it to me.

"A sound move, Eli," I said and took the map from him.

Eli continued to outline directions as I studied the crude map, "I seem to recall an old abandoned line shack a few miles beyond where I had to turn back. I think that they are holding Laura there."

Eli's description sounded vaguely familiar and I said so, "I seem to recall that area from my previous travels also. Clay, let's get mounted, there's a party to attend and we're running late."

Laura's boys looked hopeful as we hit the saddle and rode out the gates toward the northwest.

*   *   *

It had been two days since Laura was forcefully taken from the Sumner spread. Presently, the kidnappers held her in a shack hidden in the foothills to the Rockies. She was free to move about, but locked in a small back room. From the first, Laura searched for a way out with no success. The room was sparse, yet she made do for her comfort. Periodically, she paced back and forth searching for possibilities to break loose from their clutches.

Supper, such as it was, came to a nightstand beside the rickety bunk nailed to the wall. Beans and fatback bacon lay alongside a chuck of hardened bread in the tin plate. Strong coffee came to her in a tin cup. The meager meal seemed gross; however, she was hungry and ate it anyway. It left an unpleasant taste in her mouth.

Laura surmised that her captors would be forced to turn their backs on her sooner or later. Hopefully there would be a horse close by. Laura prayed that her foreman, Judd Ellison, would notify Cole Stockton. She knew also that the outlaw plan was to kill Cole.

Laura figured that she would not be molested until Cole showed up. Following Cole Stockton's demise, the young ranch woman shuddered to think of what they planned for her—an attractive woman with a striking figure. The more Laura thought about the situation, the more she knew that she needed a way to escape her captors and make them chase her straight to Cole Stockton.

Laura listened intently at the door while the outlaws discussed their plans. Something didn't make sense. They talked about a Marshal Stockton, yet referred to the Dakota Territory. The kidnappers described the Marshal's prowess with guns and his savvy on the wild trails, speaking about how he tracked down some of their gang and shot them. That sounded just like Cole Stockton, but—was it?

The next afternoon Laura banged on the door, shouting for them to let her out; she needed some privacy outside. Wylie Thompson opened the door grinning at her wryly before turning to Shorty Knudson and another outlaw. "You two guys take this gal out to the back bushes. Mind your manners. You don't, and you'll answer to me." At least Thompson understood her predicament.

The two hard outlaws delegated to escort her were bearded and outfitted in dingy clothes. Walking between them, Laura could hardly contain herself. The stench of body odor indicated they probably hadn't washed in weeks.

Once into the underbrush, Laura stooped down pretending to do her business. She quietly eased herself from the thicket and once clear, scurried silently along the underbrush only to suddenly trip over a protruding root. She landed sprawling, face down amidst a thorny bush. Involuntarily, she cried out in pain. Realizing her misfortune, Laura quickly rose and ran down a gully.

The two men charged with watching Laura heard the outcry and knew that she was gone. They shouted the alarm to the cabin, then commenced to beat the bushes looking for her.

Laura's breath came in quick rushes, "Where are the horses?" she asked herself. Moments later, she left the gully only to stumble into a dry creek bed. "Which way?" she thought, her mind racing. "To the left. I'll run down the creek bed."

Luck was with her. Within a few yards more she came to the horse corral. Mickey stood just ahead, ears pricked up. The black sensed her urgency. Laura didn't wait to saddle, she climbed the corral bars, leaping upon Mickey's back. Grabbing mane, and guiding the horse to the far end of the corral, she heeled him straight toward the bars. Laura hung on for dear life, leaning forward as the coiled muscles of the animal sprang upward, and suddenly, with a jolt to the ground, woman and horse were running full out toward the east.

Laura chanced a quick look back to see the men saddling up for the chase. She had only minutes to put a great deal of distance between them and herself, but she trusted the black. Mickey didn't need a second invitation to move quickly.

After several minutes, Laura turned south, having a good idea where Cole Stockton would be coming from. "Can I reach him in time?" she wondered.

All seven of the gang hurriedly saddled their horses. They picked up Laura's trail within minutes. Both Sid Benton and Wylie Thompson chastised the two men for allowing Laura to slip away.

"If we don't catch that woman, you'll wish you'd never been born," yelled Sid at the men, as he sunk spur to his animal.

The outlaws surmised the ranch woman would head towards her spread. Having scouted the territory, they knew of a shorter route. They were correct. Shortly, the entire gang emerged from the tree line only a hundred yards behind Laura.

The whine of a bullet past her head caused Laura to glance at her back trail. The entire gang was gaining on her. Mickey was game but slowing down, having run the greater distance.

The gang was closing on her. Within a few minutes it would be over. Laura gritted her teeth, urging Mickey onward. She would try to the end. "I wish I had a gun," she thought.

Shorty Knudson was closing fast on Laura. The main bunch rode several yards behind him. He was grinning broadly when the heavy rifle slug took him in the chest, and he slammed backward off his mount as if hit by a hammer. He was dead before he hit the ground. The rifle report sounded a split second later, and Laura searched the distance to see two men riding hard toward her—puffs of smoke issuing from both of their rifle muzzles.

Laura slowed Mickey as she neared the approaching men. Only then did she recognize Cole Stockton. An innate sense of relief filled her senses as she asked herself, "Who is that other man with Cole? They resemble each other."

The pursuers, having seen Knutson shot out of the saddle, pulled up short and opened fire on the two men riding toward them. Dark balls of death zipped through the air searching for victims.

Cole reined in beside Laura just long enough to hand her his Winchester and several reload cartridges. "Laura, dismount and start dusting those guys. We'll take them from the sides."

Clay Stockton rode wide to the left, guiding his mount with his legs and firing both of his Colts at once into the gang. Cole rode wide to the right, firing both of his revolvers.

Laura dismounted Mickey and coaxed him to lie down so she could use him to steady the Winchester while she fired down the center of the fray.

Two more of the gang took bullets, slumping to the ground. Within minutes only three of the gang stood—Sid Benton, Wylie Thompson, and one other. Benton yelled at Clay Stockton upon recognizing him, "Get off that horse and face me you sonofabitch. I'm going to kill you."

Thompson stared at Cole Stockton, his eyes questioning, "Who are you?"

The third man dropped his guns, then squatted on the ground.

Clay Stockton dismounted the far side of his horse, flipped open the loading gate of his right hand Colt and reloaded six bullets. He stepped out from his horse—gun in hand. Benton immediately raised his pistol, aimed and fired. The bullet took Clay in the side. He winced, grabbing the wound, yet was able to thumb his Colt twice. Benton panicked at not killing Clay and fired back using a fanning technique—his bullets whining wildly all around Clay.

Momentarily, Clay fired three times in succession. All three bullets smacked into Benton's chest. The man reeled backward a few steps before crashing to the ground, his life passing before him.

Thompson made the mistake of raising his revolver toward Cole Stockton. Before he could fire, two bullets hit him in the center of his body. The outlaw jerked violently with each round as it robbed him of life. He stumbled backwards, yelling incoherently as he crumbled to the ground.

Cole walked toward him, thumbing back the hammer of his Colt for the third time. The scent of burnt gunpowder hung in the air. Thompson took his last breath, staring up the bore of Stockton's revolver.

The final member of the gang stared dumbfounded at the Marshal badges pinned on the two men. Now, he could see it; they had to be kin to each other. He raised his arms into the air, crying, "Don't shoot, I give up." A check of the others revealed three wounded men and four dead.

Cole tied up the wounded men as Clay gritted his teeth while examining his wound. He went to his saddle bags and producing a spare shirt, tore it into a pad and long strips for a bandage, wrapping it around his middle.

Silence prevailed over the scene as Laura rode up to the site, leaped off Mickey, and ran to Cole Stockton. She threw her arms around him, breathing heavily as she leaned against him with loving eyes. A full three minutes passed before they parted.

Looking first at Cole, then to Clay, Laura cocked her head to one side, questioningly. "I don't believe it! There's two of you," she exclaimed as she once again leaned against Cole.

"Laura," began Cole, "let me introduce you to my brother. Clay, meet Laura—the best damn horsewoman I've ever known, that is, save for Mother."

Laura blushed a bit, then looked again at Clay. "We'd better get you to the ranch. You need fixed up before you lose too much blood." Cole laughed good naturedly as he responded, "and some of your fine cooking with about a gallon of your hot coffee, if you please."

Laura nodded, holding back tears. Clay turned to his brother with a sly grin and drawled, "I can see why you were so anxious to get here. She's well worth the trip."

CHAPTER NINETEEN

Lambs To The Slaughter

It had been a week since my brother Clay and I arrived in the lower Colorado to find Laura Sumner riding right at us with an outlaw gang in hot pursuit. Clay was wounded slightly in the ensuing fracas. Laura was kind enough to put up with both of us until Clay was able to travel back to the Dakota Territory with his prisoners.

Not that I was anxious for my brother to go, but I wanted to spend at least a few days alone with Laura. I had been thinking seriously about our relationship these past few months. If there was a woman for me anywhere—it was Laura. She was attractive, she could cook, she could ride, and she sure could shoot. She was the epitome of a Western woman if there ever was one.

Besides, I'd been to Miller's Station, taking Clay's prisoners to the jail there with the aid of Eli Johnson. I saw a poster advertising a *Spring Fling* celebration and dance coming in two days time on the town square. The streets of town held fancy decorations with colorful bunting strung from building to building. Everyone was talking about it. Preparations, they said, were being made to lay out a plank dance floor at one end of town and to build some long picnic tables for the delicious food that was sure to come.

I wanted to ask Laura to the dance. I just needed the right time and the right place to do the asking.

We were standing at the large corral looking at the latest wild horse catch when Laura turned to me, sudden like, saying, "Let's go for a ride—alone."

I was sure willing so we saddled up Chino and that black of hers, Mickey. We rode out of her main ranch yard at an easy lope toward the creek that ran through her property.

We made small talk as we rode until finally, I just blurted it out, "Laura, there's this dance in town in two days and, I-I-I." She turned to me and with a soft smile on her face said, "Yes, Cole, I would be proud to go with you." Well, there it was—I got my answer. Laura would attend the festivities with me.

I felt as though I glowed from head to toe, and I couldn't help but to smile a silly sheepish grin. I was going to the dance with the prettiest girl in the territory.

My brother Clay departed early the next morn, anxious to get his charges back to Dakota. We said our goodbyes and promised to keep in touch better. Laura provided him a sack of meat and cheese sandwiches for the trail and even planted a farewell kiss on his cheek. I could almost swear that Clay flushed a bit. Clay's handshake with me was firm as our eyes met in mutual respect.

The following evening found Laura and me arriving at the dance in her ranch wagon. She wore a flowing sky-blue dress with dark blue velvet choker and broach. Her dark hair was put up fancy-like, and her sparkling blue eyes shined like the stars at night. It's interesting, how going to a social activity like a dance just lights up a girl's face like that. Anyway, I did my best to get duded up, just for her.

I'd donned a fresh white shirt, string tie, vest, and shined my boots. One of Laura's hands even let me splash on some of his store-bought exotic cologne. I told him that I would try it, if the men wouldn't kid me about smelling like, well, you know, something out of Tess Kearney's bawdy house. Anyway, he said it was from France, and real gentlemen over there wore it all the time. I sure didn't want to be a gentleman in France if they all smelled this way.

True to fashion, though, my Colt was strapped on. I always felt a little naked without it. Laura made me promise that I would take it off when the dance started, though, and I reluctantly agreed. I also slipped my badge into the inside pocket of my vest.

We made a right handsome couple. I noticed that there were some inquisitive glances as we arrived.

The band was warming up with a nice slow waltz so I led Laura onto the makeshift plank dance floor. I slipped my right arm around her waist and pulled her close to me. She felt soft and warm to my touch, and when I looked into those crystal blue eyes, I saw a longing there that I hadn't noticed before.

I guess you could say that I had the same longing—to hold this woman tightly in my arms and know that we were right for each other.

As the music played, we glided around the dance floor. I guess that I did all right, at least I don't recall stepping on her feet—much.

We danced until the first break when Laura went to see about the food arrangements. I went for a mug of cool beer, and to jaw a bit with the men folk. As I neared the group around the beer barrel, I overheard a man mention a word that brought chills to my spine—*sheep.*

I listened more intently now because the mere mention of sheep in cattle country brought feuding words. I certainly didn't want to be in the middle of an all out range war again. After several minutes of listening, I somewhat pieced it together.

It seemed that Ian Ferguson, a prominent rancher, had arranged to purchase a herd of sheep, and they were on the way here with a couple of Basque herders. The heated words that ensued from that point were not repeatable to respectable folk. My stand in this whole affair was simple. I would keep the peace, even if it meant shooting a few citizens to do it.

I had nothing personal against sheep; I just did not like the woolly critters all that much. However, I figured that they had a right to the grazing, same as cattle.

I would have to watch this situation very carefully. I sure didn't want to have to shoot some of these fine folks over a bunch of sheep, but I would if it came to that.

Ferguson stood his ground arguing his point for the sheep. He said that sheep and cattle could survive on the same range, and he was going to prove it by having them both on his land. "Besides," he said, "there is a good market for wool." Seeing as a goodly share of clothing in the north country was made of wool, I reckoned that he was right on that point.

The large cattle ranchers disagreed and swore an angry oath that they would put a stop to these sheep at any cost. The horse ranchers listened and stayed out of the argument. I was glad of it. I would sure hate to see Laura have to take sides.

I stepped in then and put my two cents worth into the pot. "Gentlemen, most of you know that I am Deputy United States Marshal. I want no trouble in this territory over the likes of sheep. I intend to keep the peace—at any cost. Those that cause trouble will answer to me first and then to Judge Wilkerson up at the Territorial Court."

You'd have thought that I had just beaten up on a weakling or something like that, from the searing way that they all looked at me. One gent who called himself Branson, looked at me, then in so many words told me to go and mind my own business—Marshal or not, he would act as he wished.

"Stockton," he said, "I don't care if you are a Deputy Marshal, nor do I care about your reputation with a gun. Them dammed sheep come into this territory, and I'll take good care of them. Sheep do nothing but eat up all the grass and starve cows. And, they smell like hell. So do sheep herders. So, Stockton, you just stay the hell out of this and let us ranchers deal with the problem."

I stepped up to him and held his eyes for a moment, "Branson, you are a fool. You start anything, I'll come for you and you ain't going to like it one bit."

I truly expected to have some trouble from him before this was over.

Our men folk talk was cut short when the ladies, sensing something amiss, came over and smiled. They each took our arms and led us back to the dancing. We were just in time for the next round of waltzes, ballads, and do-se-do's.

Laura walked me back to the plank dance floor, and while we were dancing a slow ballad, she leaned close to me and whispered in my ear, "What was that all about?"

"Sheep," I replied. I was going to say something else about sheep, but thought better of it, and it was a good thing I did because the next thing out of her mouth was, "What's wrong with sheep? I bought in on part of Ian's herd. I own some of those sheep coming in the next few days."

I bit my tongue to hold back the gasp that was just itching to come out. My mind, however, held no such reservations and the thought, "Holy Mother of God," flashed brilliantly before my eyes.

I'd been in some humdingers of a situation before, but now, my newly confessed feelings had just been dashed with a Texas size boulder. There was no way that I could take sides in this situation, and I suddenly feared for her safety something fierce.

It would be a very lonely stay here at Miller's Station until the fires of animosity were quelled. That there would be gunsmoke and hot lead, I was certain. I hated to do it to her, but I needed information, and I had to coax it out of her. I needed to find out when, where from, and how those sheep were coming. I decided that discretion was the better part of valor, and I would wait until the next day to begin my questioning. I surely did not look forward to it.

The rest of the dance was wonderful. I held Laura in my arms, and she kind of leaned against me. I found an intense longing for her, but in the back of my mind, the ever persistent feeling that the morrow would bring an unconditional parting kept me from expressing my true feelings for her. Tonight I felt regret that I was a Deputy U.S. Marshal.

Laura is quite uncanny at reading people so I had to shove those feelings to the bottom of my being. I wanted her, above anything else at this moment, to enjoy herself this evening. I wondered also about just how many people knew that she was a partner in this sheep deal.

Later, the picnic basket was much to my liking. Laura had packed us a passel of fried chicken, just the way I like it—crispy on the outside and juicy on the inside. There was also homemade bread with strawberry jam, and one of her deep-dish false apple pies. Of course, it weren't really apples in there, but it sure tasted like it. I must have eaten at least half of that pie by myself, and washed it down with black coffee, the kind that you could float a horseshoe in.

Later, the ride back to Laura's ranch was quiet. I could tell that she had something on her mind. She turned to me suddenly and said, "Cole, I know what is on your mind. You have to keep the peace, and here I am right in the middle of this sheep purchase. I have taken a stand because I believe in the experiment."

She continued, "You can't stay at my ranch because people would talk and say that you are siding with the sheep ranchers."

I started to say something, but she cut me off, "Damn it, Cole! Let me finish."

I shut my mouth, and she continued, "You must go tonight. But before you go, I want you to know that I like you—I like you a lot, maybe too much."

She turned her head away, and I sensed that she was crying. I pulled the team up in front of her house, and before I could get out of the wagon, tie up, and help her down, she jumped out and ran inside the house, slamming the door behind her.

I stood there a long moment in complete bewilderment. I shook my head, then took the team to the barn, and saw them stabled. I next went to the bunkhouse and picked up my trappings.

I thought, "Men, I can read. Women just naturally put me to wondering, why do they do such things?"

Even Chino got upset with me. Most probably because I rousted him out of that nice warm stall, threw my saddle on him, and started him toward the wild outdoors. He didn't take kindly toward it, and did a quick hop that I was unprepared for.

After I picked myself up off of the ground, I let him know just how upset that I was. He settled down after that, and we rode to the tree-lined slopes along the edges of Laura's ranch. I still didn't have the information needed. I would have to figure it out piece by piece. I didn't like that much.

*　　*　　*

Laura Sumner fairly jumped off the wagon before Cole Stockton could get the team halted and settled down. She dashed up the few steps to the door of her home, entered quickly, and then swung the door shut. She leaned back against the door with tears in her eyes. She had just blurted out her feelings, and also uttered the words designed to drive him off.

Now, Laura felt guilty that she didn't give Cole a chance to say anything, but she figured that it was for his own good. She honestly believed that he would spend the night in the bunkhouse, in spite of what she said. She would see him go in the morning.

Her mind reeled with thoughts. She would change her mind, she would go to him right away, and tell him she was sorry for the words that she knew hurt him. No, she couldn't do that. Cole Stockton was the law and he would have to keep the peace. Deep trouble was brewing over this sheep experiment, and now she was sorry that she had bought into it.

The young woman wanted desperately to run to Cole and throw her arms around him, to feel his strong arms around her. She wanted him to kiss her and tell her that everything would be all right. She would sleep on it, and then go to him in the morning. Everything would work out for the best.

Right then she heard the sound of hoof beats outside her open window. She rose quickly, moving to the window, and watched the lone figure of Cole Stockton ride away at a quick canter. He was going. Laura dashed to the front door and threw it open—too late. Cole was beyond calling distance. He was riding away from her.

She closed the door slowly. Big tears filled her eyes. Laura went to her bed, threw herself face down and cried, "Cole, oh Cole—if you only knew."

*　　*　　*

Chino and I spent the night in the tree line. I slept lightly, going over and over in my mind, the events of the past few days. First, the sheep were coming within a day or two. Maybe, I thought, they would get here early. I figured the direction that they would come from. I would just ride over that way to watch for them.

The next morning, I thought of going to higher ground. From an overlooking slope, I could watch the approaches to the valley area along three sides at once. "Come on Chino," I coaxed, and we started climbing the long grade up into higher country. The air was thin up there, and a cool brisk breeze was blowing—after all, this was spring.

I watched nature as I rode easy in the saddle. Twice there were mule-ear deer, then an elk, a bear family, and a lone eagle sailing on the wind. The eagle slid to a halt in midair, then dove downward to the river far below. This was nature in all its beauty.

Chino and I kept climbing until finally we reached the point that I had in mind. The panorama was breathtakingly beautiful from this vantage point. The blue sky fused with various hues of green and dark shadows of blue and purple. It formed a landscape of magnificent proportions.

I dismounted and foraged around while Chino munched on tender grass. At one place along the ledge, I found where someone had dug a fire pit to stack dry brush and fallen limbs in it. A slick canvas tarp was across the top of it, presumably to keep the wood and tinder dry. It looked a lot like a signal fire of some sort. I wondered who that someone might be and was he watching for the same thing that I was, namely a herd of sheep.

I decided to go a slight bit higher, where I could watch that place without being seen and to also keep my eyes peeled for the sheep. I led Chino to the crest, then brushed out our tracks. I picked a place hidden from view and settled down for a long wait.

It would be a cold camp, as I couldn't take the chance of building even a small fire. A fire of any size would be seen for miles around. I looked at the piece of cold beef jerky in my hand and emitted a heavy sigh. I sorely wished that it could be a large beefsteak cooked on Laura's wood stove, along with some fried potatoes, and such. Some hot coffee would be nice also. I took a big bite of the jerky and let out a long sorrowful moan.

✳   ✳   ✳

Chino and I sat slightly above the ridge of the mountain. Our wait proved shorter than I figured on. Around noontime, three riders came up the steep grade, their eyes glued on the distant passes.

I watched carefully as the three reined in around the stacked bonfire, dismounted, and hobbled their horses. They sat down on the sun-warmed ground. Two men rolled a smoke as each intently scanned the distant horizon.

The third man slipped out his revolver and played with the cylinder as though he was contemplating a shooting. That's when I recognized him. He was one of Mr. Branson's riders. The other two were not known to me, but looked to be a couple of pretty rough customers.

I contemplated their arrival when one of them jerked forward, shielding his eyes with one hand while pointing excitedly with the other. I looked hard into the direction that he was pointing, and there it was, a large white blob that seemed to flow slowly to and fro. It was a herd of sheep.

Only then did I see the container of coal oil. They were pouring it all over the stacked up tinder. A match was produced to light the bonfire. Ugly black smoke boiled up through the raging flames and the sky was filling with the *signal*. It was time.

I mounted Chino and rode forward—Winchester in hand. I was almost upon them when they turned as one. I shouted the challenge, "U. S. Marshal. Drop your gunbelts, and raise your hands. You are all under arrest."

One of the men I didn't know glared at me, then snarled, "What's the charge?"

"Lighting bonfires out of season," I retorted. Not comprehending my little joke, the look on his face was one of disbelief, and his jaw dropped open. Branson's man, however, thought differently. He was sure that he could take me. His hand flashed to lift the revolver that he played with, and I shot him straight in the middle. That heavy caliber slug slammed into his mid-section, and he jerked back and doubled over, rolling grotesquely to one side, holding his middle. Within minutes, he lay still. I surmised that he was at the gates of whichever entity won his soul.

The other two looked at the dead man, carefully unbuckled their belts and dropped them, hands rising high in the air. I dismounted the far side of Chino, watching them carefully as I slowly closed the distance between us. "Back up five paces," I commanded, and they did it, "Now, put out that fire." They immediately grabbed up handfuls of dirt, throwing it on the blaze until it was a mixture of smoldering dirt and coals. I then had them empty their canteens over it and stir it up to make sure that the fire was completely out.

Having retrieved their side arms, I slung them over their saddle horns. I turned back to the men, and said, "I'm asking two questions. One—who hired you? Two—what happens when that signal is seen?"

They owned up to it. Branson had hired them to light the signal when they saw the sheep coming. Branson and his riders would gather up all the surrounding cattlemen, and they would go out to shoot the sheep down where they found them. Last, they would just hang the herders as a lesson for all others who thought that they could bring sheep into cattle country.

Furthermore, they planned to run everyone who had anything to do with the sheep out of the territory, or bury them, and that included that woman horse rancher, Laura Sumner. There it was;

the beginnings of a range war. The killing of stock, hanging herders, mysterious shootings, and nightriders to strike terror into the hearts of all concerned. The fat was in the fire now, and I was mad as hell. I had to get to that sheep herd before the cattlemen did.

"Now what, Marshal?" asked the taller of the two men. I reached to one of their horses and took up a lariat. I tossed it to him. "Tie him up," I nodded toward the shorter one. Once that was done, I took another lariat and tied up the tall man. Then, having them sit back to back, I tied them together, saying "You two should be able to work yourselves loose in about an hour or so. After that, I want the both of you to take Branson's man to the undertaker, then get your gear from wherever you left it and light a shuck out of this Territory. Don't ever come back."

Both men nodded their understanding as I mounted, starting Chino down toward the sheep over the most direct route I could see. That route was right down the steep grade. I took a deep breath, leaned far back in the saddle, and over the ledge we went a-slipping and a-sliding.

I hadn't prayed much in a long time, but now the words flashed across my mind, "Our Father, who art in Heaven . . . ."

It seemed like an eternity, but we finally bottomed out on the floor of the valley. I breathed a sigh of relief, then touched spur to Chino's flanks. He must have read my mind because as we leveled out, he broke into the long stretch. I leaned forward in the saddle to feel his powerful muscles rippling between my legs. There is nothing like a good run to straighten out the kinks.

Ahead, I saw a rising dust cloud closing in on the sheep herd to the far right, so I set a course to intercept the cattlemen. I had no idea how I would stop them—I only knew that I had to get between those riders and the sheep.

Chino ran true, and when the cattlemen approached, I was sitting in a meadow, right there in front of them. My Winchester rested on my thigh, and a bite of tough trail jerky sat in my jaw. I was not in a good mood, and I hoped that they would see it that way.

The group pulled up short in front of me. I'd say there were about twelve men in all. I was fairly outnumbered. Taking stock of the participants, I found that Branson was not with this group, and that worried me.

The solution to this part of the problem came in a flash of brilliance. I grinned at the leader, Josh Whitman, and said, "Glad you boys are here. I need some deputies to help keep the peace and escort this sheep herd over to Ferguson's range. You'll swear in or I'll shoot you where you sit, starting with you. Raise your right hand or grab iron."

It took only a second or two for them to raise their hands—They knew me quite well. I swore the whole bunch in as Deputy U.S. Marshals, Provisional.

Now, I asked the critical question, "Where is Branson?" Whitman spoke up, "He and four others are on the way to the Sumner ranch. They said that they were going to burn her out. Marshal, we didn't want anything to do with that."

I hoped that Chino was rested enough to make good time. "You men take care of that sheep herd. I want all of it on Ferguson's range by sundown. I will meet you there." I knew that their word was their bond. These were honest men, and they would do my bidding.

I turned Chino toward Laura's place, and once again put all my faith in his strength and stamina. The big roan sensed the urgency of this ride, so we fairly ate up the miles between the cattlemen and Laura's ranch.

We were within a mile of the ranch when I saw the smoke and heard the crackle of heavy gunfire. We topped out on the slight rise above the ranch house and found the stables engulfed in flames.

Two figures were down in the front yard, and gun smoke billowed periodically from various positions inside and near the house. I anxiously watched as four men rushed the front door. The door smashed open and the men dashed into the house. Gunfire erupted sharply.

At the same time, I saw a lone figure climb out of the side rear window to start running toward the burning stables. That had to be Laura. A rifle cracked and the figure jerked suddenly and slumped to the ground.

My heart beat wildly as an anguished cry of "No!" issued from my throat.

Unconsciously I reached back and jerked my Winchester from its boot, levering a round into the chamber.

A fifth man stepped out from behind the house and the other four joined him. They walked toward the fallen figure.

Only one thing crossed my mind as I yelled, "To hell with the law—I'm going to kill all five of them!" I sunk spur to Chino causing him to jump into an all out run for the five men. I worked the lever of my Winchester, slamming deadly lead into the middle of the group, aiming quickly as I rode hell bent towards them.

One man was down—two men were down. The remaining three turned toward me, guns smoking. Molten lead zipped past my head, yet I was without fear. I didn't care. I was out to kill each and every mother's son of them.

A sudden burning sharp pain in my left side told me that I'd been hit. I gritted my teeth against the pain and emptied my rifle in the direction of the remaining three.

I was almost on them now, and drove Chino straight into one of the men. I heard bones cracking as he went down screaming under my horse.

I jumped off Chino, wincing from the pain in my left side as my feet hit the ground. I drew my right hand Colt and, once clear of the big horse, found myself facing Branson and one of his riders. I shot his man twice, then aimed at Branson himself.

His revolver was already firing and I took another one through the upper left thigh. My own Colt misfired, and I threw it at Branson. He ducked and I thrust myself at him. He went down under my momentum, and in the subsequent scuffle, he lost his revolver.

We tumbled together in a flurry of flying fists and grappling arms. I got one hand around his throat and I was choking the life out of him as he desperately tried to locate his gun.

All at once, he rammed his fist into my wounded side and I almost passed out, but somehow kept my hold on him. He slammed me again. I got really mad. I let go of his throat for an instant and smashed him straight in his face—again and again and again. I wanted to beat him to death.

I looked at his eyes and they were sheer hatred, ugly, mean. I knew immediately that the only way I could take him was to find that revolver he lost. I rolled off him to search for the gun.

Branson suddenly lunged up and knocked me off balance. I slammed to the ground and rolled over just in time to miss being boot-stomped by the man.

I tried to rise, but he kicked me in the gut. By God, it hurt like blazes, and I groaned from the pain, doubling over and holding my midsection.

Branson grinned crookedly, then laughed like a wild man. He reached behind his left hip and pulled a long razor-sharp skinning knife. His eyes glared wild and crazy as he started toward me with that knife.

I tried to roll out of his reach to catch my breath. He kicked me again, right straight in the ribs. With all my strength, I shoved myself up to my feet, staggered back, and stumbled. I went down hard, with the breath knocked out of me.

There was a sudden scuffle, and I looked up just in time to see Branson go down screaming under the hooves of a big roan horse.

The ensuing silence was deafening, as I felt Chino's wet muzzle against my face.

Painfully, I rolled over and searched the dust for the fallen figure of Laura. I crawled to her, seeing the dark red stain on the back of her shirt. With pain-filled eyes I gently took her in my arms and brushed the tosseled hair and dirt from her face.

Her eyes were closed, and her once vibrant body lay limp in my arms. I silently cursed myself for not getting here sooner—for leaving her in the first place.

It was then that I noticed the tear drop. A solitary tear drop trickled from her left eye, and ran down her dirty cheek. Dead people don't shed tears. I looked closer at her face and her lips moved in a slight whisper. I leaned closer to her face.

She opened her eyes slightly and I saw the pain in them, "You came back. I was hoping you would—they hit us with no warning. They were riding in slowly and peaceably, in the next instant they drew their guns and started shooting. Oh, God, my back hurts. Where is Branson?"

"Dead," I answered dryly. "Don't you die on me now! I've got to get us up to the house and figure out how to get help."

My thoughts were answered with the drumming of hooves. Ian Ferguson, some of his riders, and about a half dozen of my "deputies" came galloping into the ranch yard.

"Damn," I heard Ferguson say. "It looks like a massacre." I shouted to him with a painfully weak voice, and they rode over to us. Suddenly, hands were gently lifting Laura from me. Others helped me to my feet. They took us into the house. Two more of Laura's ranch hands were inside, alive.

They took Laura back to her room and laid her on her bed. Ferguson sent a rider for the doctor. He told me that the sheep had gotten to his place and that's when they saw the smoke from the barn and decided not to wait for me to show up. Most of his words passed through my mind as unintelligent garble as I passed out from sheer exhaustion and the pain in my side.

A day or two later when I finally opened blurry eyes to a sunlit room, I lay there a minute or two to let them focus. Everything was hazy. I took a long deep breath. I was alive. My eyes wandered around the room. It was then I realized that I was lying on a makeshift cot in Laura's living room. Two more men were stretched out on similar cots across the room from me.

I remembered that Laura had been shot, and I moved to get up out of bed. I was stiff and sore, and bandaged up around my chest and thigh. I managed to sit up, but my head was reeling. Someone came into the room, and a woman's voice shouted,

"The Marshal's awake, he's up, come and help me."

More people came into the room, and I looked up into the smiling faces of Ian Ferguson and his wife, Molly, along with Judd Ellison, Eli Johnson, and Mike Wilkes.

"Welcome back, Marshal," said Ferguson. "You had us worried for a while."

"Where is Laura?"I hoarsely inquired.

"She's in her room, Cole. She lost a lot of blood, but she is fine now, thanks to your arrival. We buried the dead, and rounded up all of Laura's stock, including her black horse, Mickey."

"Take me to her," I commanded, and they helped me up and shuffled me to Laura's room. I stood in the doorway looking at her. She was sleeping, and the light from the window fell softly across her face. Her long dark hair fell loosely on the pillow. She was alive. I couldn't help it, tears rolled down my cheek.

I moved to step toward her and staggered. Friends moved to help me, but I motioned them off. I had to walk to her on my own.

My shuffling wakened her, and she turned to face me, her eyes anxiously searching mine. A smile formed on her mouth as I slowly limped and shuffled to her side. I hurt like hell, but nothing was going to keep me from doing what I had to do.

I kneeled on the floor beside her, took her hand in mine, bent over, then gently kissed her waiting lips. It would be a long time before I left her side again. Behind me, I heard Molly Ferguson tell the others, "Come, we are not needed here."

CHAPTER TWENTY

Disaster On The Mountain

With heavy rains in the mountain passes recently, the crusty old coach driver was forced to pick his way cautiously along the steep ledge of the pass. The passengers, two women and three men, were talking to one another.

The stagecoach rounded the curve slowly in the pass when several feet of erosion gave way. Suddenly, the vehicle lurched toward the open edge of the cliff and the driver was thrown into empty space, shrieking as he fell.

The six-horse team unnerved by the sudden lurch tried to bolt, but stumbled to their knees, and the heavy wagon leaned into the sliding mud wash. Within brief seconds, the entire coach, and team, slipped off the mountain—tumbling over and over in a death roll for the canyon floor.

Screams of passengers and horses alike went unheeded except to the wild critters of the mountain as they crashed to a sudden stop on rocky ground four hundred feet below. Stillness followed.

Half a day later, a lone figure emerged from the wreckage. A young woman had miraculously been cushioned among the other passengers, suffering minor injuries and a concussion that left her without a memory and a name.

She sat dazed beside the coach for an hour or so, then rose and rummaged around the smashed wagon. Finding a single canteen of water, she drank the warm life giving liquid. Disoriented, she faced toward the afternoon sun and began walking slowly—to where, she did not know.

*   *   *

Three months had passed since Cole Stockton and Laura Sumner were wounded in the sheep episode. Both healed rather quickly, and Cole spent a good deal of time helping out on the Sumner ranch. Laura knew, however, that something was on his mind.

One day, without much notice, Cole just up and rode over to the Territorial Seat to speak with Judge Wilkerson. He returned with a somewhat empty look about him. It took Laura Sumner all of about thirty minutes to realize that he must have resigned as Deputy U. S. Marshal.

He wasn't wearing the badge anymore, and he put on a good show of learning the horse ranching business. Laura knew him pretty well by this time. It just wasn't like Cole to be a rancher. Marshalling was his calling, and she dearly wished that he would realize that truth and go get his badge back; none-the-less, she knew this was something that he had to work out for himself.

Laura prayed that she was not the reason for him turning in the star.

*   *   *

Cole and I were sitting on the porch of my house having a cup of coffee when a dust cloud in the distance caught our attention. We watched attentively while the rumbling farm wagon ambled toward us.

The closer the wagon came, the more anxious Cole became. It was as if a foreboding sense had suddenly enveloped him with a dark veil. I watched his face as he became intensely interested in the occupants of the wagon.

When the wagon finally entered the ranch yard, Cole immediately put his coffee down, stood up, and stepped off the porch to meet with these folks. By the looks of their clothing they were farmers.

Cole seemed to know the couple, so I rose to move to his side as he listened intently to what the folks had to say. I searched the eyes of the woman, and they were filled with tears. The husband had worried eyes and asked him if he would help them find someone.

Cole turned to me and said, "Laura, these folks are Vern and Lucy Miller. They rode all the way from Creede to see me. Their daughter, Allison, is sixteen now. A few days ago, she was riding the coach to visit some friends up in Cheyenne. The coach met with an accident, going over the edge of a cliff. All were killed except Allison, and now she is missing."

Cole continued, "They believe that she somehow crawled out of the wreckage and is now on foot, probably lost. Footprints were found, but the rescuers lost the trail a few hundred yards away over rocky ground. These folks are mighty worried about her. They have asked for my help to track her down and bring her back."

I thought immediately, "This was just the thing that Cole needs to bring him to his senses. He must remember that his calling and duty is to serve and protect the people of the Colorado Territory."

Locating and rescuing Allison was a job that I knew he had to take. I immediately offered my opinion, "Cole. You must go. She needs a friend, someone she knows, to find her. You know that territory. It is wild, and there are those that would harm her—outlaws, Indians and even wild animals. Yes, Cole, you must go."

I sensed his relief as I spoke my mind, although, I also sensed that he wished he could stay with me. I gave him a reassuring smile, then took his face in my hands. I looked deeply into those blue-green eyes, and transmitted my thoughts to him. That was something that we often did. We could read each other's eyes to know what the other was thinking.

We had grown that way from our first meeting a year and a half ago. My mind flashed back to the morning that he limped and shuffled his way to my bed after both of us were wounded by ruthless men. I knew that he dearly wanted to ask me to marry him. As we kissed, we silently spoke to each other with our eyes and I told him that we should wait.

I would always be his best friend, and that seemed to sit right with both of us. Silently, he promised to always be at my side when I needed him. I believed that things would be all right, although I knew in the back of my mind that the wild trails would always be in the back of his.

Yes, Cole Stockton was right for Marshalling. He had a sense about him of right and wrong, and a certain stubbornness to see things through. There were those who feared him, but there were also those who respected him, and of course those that loved him, and I was one of these. I am probably the closest person to him.

We spoke and decided that the farm couple should stay with me on my horse ranch for a few days. Besides, I had some things that needed fixing—wagons, harnesses and such. Cole knew Vern was quite the handyman when it came to fixing things; I should hire him to take care of chores while he was on the trail. I knew exactly what he meant. The Millers were down on their luck and could sure use the money. Besides, I knew he felt good about them keeping me company.

Cole planned to get an early start in the morning, so we spent the remainder of the evening together after the Millers retired to a spare bedroom. We sat on the settee in front of the fireplace with the glow of the smoldering coals casting eerie shadows on the walls.

I lay my head on his shoulder and his arm went around me. I looked up into his face and there was that unmistakable sparkle in his eyes again. I knew that he was already on the trail in his mind, and I snuggled closer to him, not wanting the morning to come too quickly.

*   *   *

The breaking dawn brought an overcast and dismal day, and I hoped for the Millers' sake that this was not an omen of what might come. Lucy and I rustled up food supplies for Cole to take with him, as well as preparing a hearty breakfast to start his day out right.

Vern Miller helped him gear up his packhorse. Vern related details to Cole of how Allison looked now, as well as little stories of her "growing up."

Suddenly, Vern turned to Cole, his eyes red with tears and cried out with trembling voice, "Either way, Cole, we've got to know." Cole somberly nodded his understanding.

I packed a lunch of bread and sliced beef for later on, then walked with Cole to the front porch. He checked the gear on Chino, put the lunch into a saddlebag, then turned to me. His eyes met mine and quickly our arms were around each other. He whispered into my ear, "I'll be back—soon."

Then he turned, and with foot to stirrup, off he rode at a steady pace as the Millers stood holding each other. I whispered softly into the light breeze, "Find her and bring her back, Cole."

The Millers and I watched until Cole Stockton disappeared from our view.

CHAPTER TWENTY-ONE

Cole's Quest

I rode away from Laura's ranch with my mind chock full of inconsistent thoughts. It was hard watching Laura get shot down by Branson, and at that moment, I did something that ran against my grain. I purposely forgot that I was *The* Law. In a fit of obvious revenge, I wanted to kill those men responsible.

Later, seeing Laura lying there in that soft glow of sunlight, I felt a strange sense of guilt come over me. If I hadn't left her in the first place, she wouldn't have been shot. I silently vowed to make things right for her.

I felt that I couldn't do that as Deputy U. S. Marshal and rode over to see Judge Wilkerson. I tried to resign, but he wouldn't hear of it. He made a good argument for me to keep the badge, and placed me on what he called an *inactive* status until—well, whenever I took it upon myself to pin the silver star back on.

Vern and Lucy Miller, whom I'd met in Creede a few years earlier, came to me with a dilemma. Their sixteen-year-old auburn-haired daughter had disappeared from a stagecoach accident and was presumably lost and wandering alone in the wilds of the Colorado Territory. They asked for my help in tracking her down and bringing her back home.

On one hand, I felt obligated to stay and watch out for Laura's well being. On the other hand, no matter what I had promised myself, I had to help these people. I couldn't turn them down. Either way I looked at the situation, it became something that I had to do. I had to prove myself worthy again.

Chino and I arrived at the stagecoach wreckage site to find that the rescuers had certainly made a mess of any clues that might have been. I had to piece this situation together step-by-step and start thinking like a stunned and frightened person.

"Where would I go? Which way would I go? Who am I? Where do I belong?" These questions surged through my mind as I pondered my next actions.

I was told that the accident happened in the late morning. I figured that the lone survivor would want to travel with the sun. I remounted Chino and with packhorse in tow, we started westward, riding slowly and watching for sign. I found the trail of the rescue party and followed it until it petered out with rocky ground.

I dismounted and walked around for a while, searching for something out of the ordinary—an overturned rock, a slight imprint on moss, anything that might have been overlooked by the rescue group.

From here, the terrain sloped upward, and once again I had to think, "If I were Allison and walking, would I go up the rocky ground, or along the side of the slope?"

I figured it more difficult to walk along the side of the slope and selected the rocky way. I went upward over the rocky ground, Chino and the packhorse slowly picking their way—me, looking for some sign that I was right.

I'd heard from good trackers that the way to find something is to look for what should be there, not for what isn't supposed to be there. I hoped that they were right, because a half mile further, I found some overturned rocks, like someone stumbled, and dislodged them.

A ride further up slope turned up a jagged torn piece of light blue calico. I thought perhaps, it might be a piece of the dress that Allison wore. I tucked it in my coat pocket. I rode forward, still searching intently until darkness prevailed. I decided to make camp under a cluster of pines. Scooping out a circle of earth with my hunting knife, I built a fire to brew Arbuckle's coffee and warm some beans and bacon in a small skillet. There was an even greater reason for letting that fire burn bright. A campfire can be seen for miles in darkness. I thought, even wished a bit, that Allison might see my fire and turn toward me. I had no way of knowing if it would work, but the glow of my fire might turn the odds of rescue in her favor.

I ate the meager meal reflecting on that which I had found. I believed that I had her direction, and now I needed another clue to confirm that I was indeed on her trail. I let the fire die down and rolled up in my blankets. I dozed lightly with my Colt at hand, and it felt reassuring.

Unconsciously, once again I attuned myself to the wilds of the Colorado. A man cannot enter and sustain himself within the realm of nature without nature becoming one with him. When that happens, he knows the sounds and silences of the trail as well as the meaning behind them. And so it was with me this night.

The morning brought sunlight and warmth to the hills. Rousting up Chino and the packhorse, we broke camp and continued the hunt for Allison Miller. I chewed on buffalo jerky while I rode a slow zigzag pattern continually searching the ground for clues that I was on the right track. Several hours into my ride I found another piece of that same blue calico.

The material proved that I was definitely on her trail now. The land now sloped downward into a long valley. I paused a moment to survey the land and it was a good thing I did, because a movement to the far right caught my eye. A group of renegade Cheyenne moved slowly along the slope below me. I figured them for a hunting party.

I wanted no trouble at this point, so I quickly moved into a stand of pines—Winchester at the ready. Chino stood still while I waited impatiently for them to ride out of my view. I never moved for what seemed thirty minutes or so longer. Then, I rode steadily forward down the slope, being careful to watch my back trail. A village of Indians moving is one thing, but a hunting party could change direction at any moment. I didn't want to worry about someone coming behind me at this time.

Around noon, I found the remains of a campsite. I read the sign. It appeared to me that the girl had stumbled into this camp, and met up with someone. I found the tracks of one mule, one large man, and of smaller footprints, possibly the girl.

They left together it seemed and had turned north. By the spacing of foot and hoof prints, they were traveling slowly. The northerly direction was bad news to me. They were moving even further into Indian territory. If they continued that direction, they could eventually run into a party of Cheyenne or Arapaho.

Up to this point, I felt quite sure that Allison was all right. At least no apparent harm had come to her. I surmised that I was within a day of her, the morrow would prove that.

Once again darkness fell, but this time, I was certain that I was on the right track, and I settled down to thinking about Laura again. What was it about her that melted my resolve? I'd known a few women before, but none like her. Laura seemed to know my mind like she was a part of my very soul. She just naturally made me feel at ease. She knew my wild side as well as how to light my internal fires.

I was a drifter, a lawman born to the gun, and I sometimes needed to be alone for quiet reflection on my past. She knew me and accepted me as I was, and that was why she was in my mind.

Mid-morning the following day brought an alarming situation. The prints I was following showed longer strides between the imprints. That told me that they were moving faster. I topped the next rise and pulled up short. The far side of the hill was littered with camping and prospecting equipment. At the bottom of the hill, I found the body of a bewhiskered old prospector, and the carcass of a dead mule. Both had been shot several times.

Shod hoof prints and deep boot marks amongst the churned up ground told the tale. The prospector and young woman had come across a group of horsemen, and I estimated about five in all. Allison was now in the clutches of vicious men, and I feared for her safety.

The trail appeared not more than a few hours old. I had to hurry now. "Come on, Chino," I said anxiously. The big roan horse responded with a quickening of his stride, the packhorse running to keep up.

Their trail was easy to follow. They rode straight and steady to the west. Two hours later brought specks in the distance. It was time. I reached into the inside pocket of my coat. My fingers touched the silver star of Deputy U. S. Marshal. The decision came quick. I pinned the *Sign of the Law* onto my shirt front.

An old stirring surged through my body, and Chino sensed it. His pace increased as my hand slid back to the stock of my Winchester. Withdrawing it from the scabbard, I levered a round of 44.40 into the chamber.

I was only fifty yards from them when they noticed me. I slowed to a walk, allowing the pack animal to fall back to its usual pace while I watched the men carefully.

Yes, the girl was being held by one of them. I rode closer. Allison looked haggard in that torn and tattered blue calico dress. There was fear and defeat on her dirty face.

I rode right up to about ten yards of them, and they spread out. I said nothing, but looked intently at each man's face, searching out each man's intentions. A moment later, one man's face reflected an instant recognition, and blurted out, "Stockton! Cole Stockton!"

His hand flashed for the gun at his belt. With no recourse, I shot him straight in the middle. That opened the ball. Each man reached for his weapons, and I worked the lever of that Winchester as fast as I could. They scrambled everywhere. In spite of her stupor, Allison screamed and cowered in terror.

I dismounted the far side of Chino and dropped my empty rifle to the ground. Suddenly two Colts were in my hands, speaking the sound of authority. I stepped toward them cocking and firing my revolvers one after the other. Smoke and hot lead burst from the muzzles.

Three of the men were down and either dead or dying. Bullets ripped up the earth all around me. Moulton lead whistled past my ear, past my body, and I truly expected to get hit.

At not more than five yards, I stood with legs planted firmly on the ground, waiting for the burning pain that I knew was coming. Carefully I chose my targets, and squeezed off that .44 caliber death and destruction.

It was easy to see that these men had never faced a true gunfighter, one who would just stand there, ready to take lead and keep shooting back.

Now, there were two left standing. One of these men held Allison in front of himself as a shield. He shouted to me, "Drop your guns, Marshal, and I'll let the girl live."

He was much larger than the girl, however, so I took careful aim and pulled the trigger. The second man dropped his gun and fell to the ground begging for his miserable life.

Allison crumbled to her knees, trembling all over, the dead man's blood spattered all over the back of her hair and dress. She sobbed uncontrollably, tears streaking down her grimy face.

I walked up to the man on ground, cocked the hammer on my Colt, and placed the hot steel bore against his forehead. "I am Cole

Stockton, Deputy United States Marshal. You are under arrest for the murder of the prospector and the kidnapping of this girl. You'll come peaceably, or I'll leave your dead carcass for the buzzards."

The man decided quickly to come along. I went to Chino for a set of handcuffs, then secured him for the moment. Then, I knelt beside Allison, touched her shoulder gently, and spoke softly to her, "Allison, everything is all right now. I am here to take you home."

CHAPTER TWENTY-TWO

Resurrection And Faith

Back at the Sumner ranch, Laura contemplated the situation. "Cole had been gone four full days so far. Evening was always the loneliest part of the day for me when Cole was away on the trails." I wondered, "Was he safe? Had he found Allison? Was he thinking about me? Of us?"

With supper and kitchen chores out of the way, I slipped out to the porch with a cup of coffee. Lucy Miller presently joined me on the porch and looked up into the sky. "Cole is a good man," she said suddenly. "We just don't know what we would've done without his help. I wish that there were more lawmen like him. It would be a better place for everyone."

I turned to her replying, "He's out there because he is a good lawman, but above that, he is Cole Stockton, a man that uses his special talents for the good of mankind. He knew that he was the right man for the job, no matter the outcome."

Lucy nodded half-heartedly, emitted a long sigh, and went back inside the house to sit with Vern. I silently prayed that Cole had found Allison, and that he would be back soon. Without warning, an affirmation flooded over my being. It was at that very instant, that I somehow knew that Cole was on his way back to us. As to when they would come riding into the ranch yard, I had no idea. I just knew that he was working his way back. Pangs of anxiety battled my relief and grabbed deep within my heart.

The fifth day came and went. Still, there was no sign of Cole and Allison. No matter what I was doing or how much I tried, I couldn't keep myself from periodically searching the horizon for some sign of them. It was like I half way expected them to come riding over the rise in front of the ranch at any moment.

Occasionally, my thoughts turned to dismal visions. "What if Cole is in trouble?" I asked myself, "What if he was lying out there in the wilds shot up, or worse, lying dead on the cold ground?" I wondered, "Would some kind passing stranger take the time to bury him and mark the grave to be found some time in the future?" Try as I might, these images were indelible in my mind.

"No!" I told myself. My positive thoughts were true. "He is on his way back and he will be here sometime tomorrow." I felt the tear roll out of my eye and slowly trickle down my cheek. I brushed it away with my hand but more tears flooded my eyes. I sat down on the porch steps holding my head in my hands, silently weeping to myself. I felt tired and helpless. After several minutes, I left the porch and went to my bed. Images of a savage wilderness filled my mind until I slipped into fitful slumber.

$$* \quad * \quad *$$

Allison looked up at me with a flood of tears bursting from her big brown eyes. The spark of recognition was there. Evidently, the events of the past few minutes had stirred her memory. She struggled to stand on weak and wobbly legs.

I rose and pulled her up gently. She threw her arms around my neck, holding onto me tightly. She had indeed grown up. Leaning against me, she repeated my name in between sobs of obvious relief at being found by someone she knew and trusted.

"Mr. Stockton," she sobbed. "I thought that I would never see home again. Thank you for coming for me."

I had no doubts what the group of men had in mind for her. I silently thanked the good Lord that I was able to get here when I did. It was a long way back to Laura's ranch, and I wanted to get there as quickly as possible. However, I had a live prisoner, and four dead men to account for.

It was four days back to the ranch, and two days back to the Territorial Seat and Judge Wilkerson's jail. I chose the jail route, and decided to take the bodies back with us. I had the prisoner help me lash the bodies to their horses.

Our procession entered the city of Denver two days later. People stopped their activities, lining up along the streets as we passed by. Allison rode beside me with the handcuffed prisoner on his animal behind me. I lead his mount. The remainder of our element was a train of horses roped to each other with blanket-covered bodies tied over each saddle. Our trek ended in front of the Territorial Jail. Deputies emerged from the stone building and relieved me of my prisoner as well as the string of burdened horses.

I escorted Allison to my boarding house and introduced her to Ma Sterling who took charge and immediately ushered her to a hot soapy bath. Ma suggested that I not return for some three or four hours. As Ma put it, "This poor child will be bathed, rested, have a fresh dress, and fed properly before the likes of Deputy Marshal Cole Stockton sees her again. I recollect a trunk in the storage room with appropriate hand-me-downs that should fit her. Now shoo! Off with you! I've got chicken to fry, taters to cook, and biscuits to bake. That child has probably not eaten anything more than cold jerky, knowing you Marshals like I do." I took the hint and left for Judge Wilkerson's office. There was no arguing with Ma Sterling when she set her mind to things.

Once again, my arrival in Denver had already been announced to the judge. Henry, the clerk, ushered me straightaway into his office. Judge Wilkerson rose as I entered, once again wearing the *Star of Justice*. He had a sly grin on his face. I guess he had me figured from the start. Marshalling was in my blood now, and forever would be. It struck me then that Laura knew it, too.

"Marshal Stockton," he said, "it is very good to see you again. I have already been informed of your entourage. Come. Sit down. Tell me the circumstances."

Over the next hour or so I told the story of the coach accident, of the Millers' request, and of tracking Allison's trail. I related the murder of the old prospector and subsequent kidnapping of Allison as well as the final shoot out. Judge Wilkerson nodded his understanding of each detail with intense interest. In the end, he stood and held out his hand to me, "Marshal Stockton, I knew what kind of man you were when I first summoned you to join my group. You have not let me down. I hereby detail you to escort the young lady home to her parents. No doubt you also have a special friend anxiously awaiting your return." And then, a warm look came over his face as he motioned me out the door.

*   *   *

It was Sunday, nine days since Cole rode out to the wilds in search of Allison Miller. The Millers and I were all on edge, continually watching the horizon, praying for a dust cloud—praying for that speck that foretold of his coming.

I dressed in one of Cole's favorite dresses, the flowered print that I wore the first time we parted. I even took the time to put my hair up the way that he liked it, and the coffee was on the stove—just the way he liked it, strong and black.

Lucy Miller sat on the porch rocking back and forth and staring at the distant horizon. Vern Miller sat on the bottom step aimlessly whittling on a stick. Silent prayers drifted up on the gentle breeze that blew strands of my dark hair in front of my eyes.

It was unusually warm for this part of the year. Glimmering heat waves danced in the distance, making our eyes strain and smart to remain focused for more than a few minutes at a time.

A tiny dark speck suddenly appeared far in the distance. It moved slowly. We concentrated on it with restless breath, fearful to even wish.

The speck grew larger. It was one rider. No! There were two riders—two riders and a packhorse. The silhouettes of a man and a woman came into view. It was Cole Stockton and Allison.

I looked over to Lucy Miller as she rose slowly from the rocker. She trembled and cried uncontrollable tears that flooded her cheeks. I looked down at Vern Miller. He too rose, to find his wife beside him. He removed his battered old hat—tears of joy streaming down his weathered face. They moved as one toward Cole and Allison as they rode into the ranch yard.

I stood speechless, with trembling legs and watery eyes as the two stopped. A sobbing Allison was tenderly lifted from her horse by her father's loving hands, then enveloped once again into the waiting arms of both her parents.

Cole sat his roan watching them for a long minute, then—he looked up and our eyes met.

He dismounted from Chino and began what seemed an eternal stroll toward me—his eyes never leaving mine.

Sunlight glinted on the *Silver Star* pinned to his shirtfront.

I rushed to him and felt his arms move around me, pulling me closer, holding me tightly. I looked up into his loving eyes, and everything was right between us.